Ride for the
Lone Star

Ride for the Lone Star

A Western Quest Series Novel

Stephen L. Turner

SANTA FE

Sunstone books may be purchased for educational, business, or sales promotional use. For information please write: Special Markets Department, Sunstone Press, P.O. Box 2321, Santa Fe, New Mexico 87504-2321.

Book and Cover design › Vicki Ahl
Body typeface › Book Antiqua
Printed on acid free paper

Library of Congress Cataloging-in-Publication Data

Turner, Stephen L., 1957-
  Ride for the Lone Star / by Stephen L. Turner.
    p. cm. -- (The Western quest series ; v. 4)
  ISBN 978-0-86534-768-7 (pbk. : alk. paper)
  1. Scots-Irish--United States--Fiction. 2. Texas--Annexation to the United States--Fiction. 3. Mexican War, 1846-1848--Fiction. I. Title.
  PS3620.U76596R53 2010
  813'.6--dc22
                                    2010025087

Published in

WWW.SUNSTONEPRESS.COM
SUNSTONE PRESS / POST OFFICE BOX 2321 / SANTA FE, NM 87504-2321 /USA
(505) 988-4418 / ORDERS ONLY (800) 243-5644 / FAX (505) 988-1025

Dedication

THIS BOOK IS DEDICATED to the memory of the late Elmer Kelton who died while this book was being written. Mr. Kelton profoundly influenced my writing. He wrote the way I think and speak. He was blessed with the ability to tell a story that few others possess.

Foreword

IN VOLUME ONE OF THE Western Quest Series, *Out of the Wilderness*, the odyssey of the Turner family in America began with the story of Thomas Turner's immigration from Ireland to South Carolina in 1749. In volume two, *On the Camino Real*, the story continues with his grandson, Aaron Turner. The young man falls under the spell of the mysterious, beautiful Spanish province of Texas. He and his companions succeed in their struggle to establish a new home for themselves on the edge of Austin's Colony on the Camino Real.

Volume three, *Under Troubled Skies*, follows the struggles of Aaron, his family and friends to sustain themselves in an increasingly dangerous time, culminating in the Texas War of Independence. This fourth volume, *Ride for the Lone Star*, completes the story of Aaron Turner's life and times during the days of the Republic of Texas and the subsequent war between Mexico and the United States. Texas was in chaos during the days of the Republic. The Indian wars raged in every corner of Texas, while the Mexicans continued to threaten Texas from the south.

The style of this fourth book differs somewhat from the previous ones. The scope of the story makes it difficult to place the protagonist at all the important events of the day so there is more narrative and less dialogue. The tone of this book is also somewhat darker than its predecessors. But those were dark days in Texas.

Ride for the Lone Star, is a work of historical fiction, as are the others in the series and the details of Aaron Turner's actual involvement in most of the events portrayed in the books are speculative. The historical record only supports that Aaron Turner was a cotton planter and stock producer on the Navasota River in what was later known as Leon County. The dates of his birth, death, marriage, and children's births are known.

Land records indicate the location of the acreage. They also show that Aaron was a slave holder, a part of the record I have chosen to edit. Leon County did not exist at the time of the Republic. It was formed later from what was Robertson County. However, to avoid confusion, the author refers to Leon County as it is known today. Records also confirm Aaron Turner's presence in that location as an ordained Methodist minister. The reader is asked to remember that this is a work of historical fiction and not a history book.

Acknowledgement

THIS BOOK WOULD NOT have been possible without help and encouragement from others. Special gratitude is due to the late Ed S. Turner of Tularosa, New Mexico, for the invaluable family historical information he compiled. Thanks are due to Ella Turner Bullard of Cross Plains, Texas, for her meticulous compilation of genealogical details. Thanks are due to my parents, Aaron Lynn Turner and Alene Turner of Sulphur Springs, Texas, for their patient proofreading and encouragement. Special thanks are due to my wife, Roberta, without whom I could do little. Finally, thanks are due to Sunstone Press of Santa Fe, New Mexico, for their continued confidence and support of my writing.

1

May 18, 1836, Louisiana Landing, Republic of Texas

THE LATE AFTERNOON SUN shone in oppressive heat through the humid air as the *Brazos Belle* approached her moorings at Louisiana Landing. As Captain Robert Contois expertly guided the tidy steamship to her berth, a cloud of dust caught his eye to the north along the river. He caught a glimpse of mounted Indians galloping down the wagon road that followed the river. A flash of color indicated painted men and horses.

"We got trouble. I'm backing water to the middle of the river. Get your rifles and get back to the pilothouse on the double!"

He sounded the piercing steam whistle to shriek out a warning to the inhabitants of Louisiana Landing: seven short blasts followed by a long continuous blast. People began to appear from the fields and on the porches. Using a speaking trumpet, he hailed the shore. "Indians to the north! Indians to the north!"

As he resumed the steam powered warning, the settlement burst into activity. Those working in the fields dropped their tools and ran for safety in William

Applewhite's fortified home or the small stockade on the Camino Real.

There was no time to unhitch the livestock. They were left harnessed to their plows and cultivators. The valuable breeding stock remained in their pasture along the river.

As the last of the slaves reached the Applewhite's house, the Indians were in sight from the doors and windows. There were at least fifty Comanche in full war dress riding painted ponies, accompanied by several Kiowa who could be distinguished by their uniquely braided hair.

Guns protruded from every rifle port of the large two story house. Thirty men and women, both black and white, stood ready to repel the expected attack.

The stockade stood one hundred yards to the south where the road met the ferry and steam boat landing. Four stone cabins with clay tile roofs were joined by stout log palisades to create a small sturdy fort. The guns of thirty-two settlers bristled from the rifle ports of the protective walls.

The *Brazos Belle* floated midstream in the safety of the muddy water. Captain Rob and his crew of five men stood armed with rifles in the pilot house. They were only fifty yards from the river bank where they could help defend both the stockade and the Applewhite house.

Joining Rob in the pilot house was his wife, Stephanie, armed with a .50 caliber rifle. She could shoot as well as most men. Their two sons, Charles and Sam, took refuge lying on the cypress pilot house deck.

The war band swarmed over the settlement gathering up all the loose livestock. They took time to cut the harness off the frightened mules in the fields, driving them away with the horses.

They pillaged the out buildings and slave cabins. Using the smoldering embers under the iron pots in front of the cabins, the Comanche set fire to the cabins. They carried fire to every barn and shed in the settlement.

The whooping Indians drove the stolen livestock north along

the river road, knowing the settlers dared not pursue them. Not a shot had been fired, not a life had been lost.

As darkness gradually descended on the decimated settlement, the defenders held their ground. Smoke lay in a choking blanket over the smoldering ruins of what had been a prosperous community. The milk cows lowed as they wandered aimlessly finding no one to milk them.

A blood curdling war cry pierced the smoky gloom as dozens of Indians appeared on foot from the north, south, and east. They were on both porches of the Applewhite's house with huge stone clubs battering the heavy oak doors. They grabbed the barrels of a few guns before they could be fired and jerked them through the rifle ports.

As quickly as the rifles had been taken, deadly saddle pistols took their place. The heavy loads of buckshot and musket balls belched death from the .69 caliber pistols. As soon as they were fired, others were immediately handed to the defenders at the gun ports.

As the defensive effort became suddenly more effective, many of the Indians were driven away from the house. This gave the settlers fighting from the house the opportunity to switch from pistols to shotguns. Deadly double barreled loads of buckshot drove them further from the house. The rifles from the second story now found targets as the Indians retreated to the safety of the darkened forest.

All through the long night the defenders of the house, stockade and steamer stood to their posts, praying for daylight. The rising sun showed blood stains on the porch and the ground near the Applewhite's house, but not a body was to be seen. The Indians had taken their dead and wounded with them.

Smoke hung heavily over the still bottom land as the embers of the cabins and barns smoldered. The coals glowed hotly beneath a blanket of ashes.

Scattered chickens scratched aimlessly for bugs and seeds. The few milk cows had paired up with their calves and were grazing near the river.

Mr. Applewhite carefully emerged from his house under the cover of many protective rifles. Blake Lane appeared from the stockade and slowly walked toward Mr. Applewhite. Captain Rob rowed a small boat from the steamer to the dock, leaving her safely anchored in the river. Rifles from the stockade and steamer covered them both. Joining up near the house, the three men made a cautious search of the area.

Finding no signs that the Comanche remained, they signaled for several of the other men to join them. They left plenty of able fighters behind to protect their families who remained within bolted doors.

They spread out into a skirmish line and cautiously walked north through the woods along the river. The *Brazos Belle* steamed slowly up river in tandem with the men on shore. The rifles in the pilot house could provide a cross fire if one was needed.

Soon they reached a clearing where the invaders had camped. The Comanche and Kiowa were gone along with the stolen livestock. In relief and frustration, the men of Louisiana Landing quickly returned to their scarred settlement.

———

The morning of May 19, 1836, broke over Fort Parker on the upper reaches of the Navasota River. The red tinted dawn reflected on the dew covered grass. It was a good day to work in the fields surrounding the fort.

It was a sturdy fort with six cabins built into the twelve foot tall log palisades with projecting blockhouses on opposite corners for added protection. It had been built a few years earlier by the extended family and friends of Elder John Parker. Parker was the leader of the Pilgrim Predestination Baptist Church which comprised the residents of the community. The fort sheltered the lives of almost fifty residents of all ages.

The fertile river bottom land was boot-top tall in corn. The oats were bleaching in the sun nearly ready to harvest. Most of the men had left at daylight to hoe or plow their corn fields. The women went about their various morning chores.

A group of six mounted Indians materialized from the mists and shadows of the forest bordering the fields. They rode slowly to the fort with a white rag tied to a gun held high above a young Indian's head.

They stopped fifty yards from the open gates of the fort. Benjamin Parker looked up from shoeing a horse inside the fort to see the danger. The Comanche and their horses were painted for war. Beyond them he could see a much larger body of Indians partially concealed in the edge of the trees.

He yelled at his wife to gather up the children and escape through the small back gate. He told her to warn the others and hide in the thickets along the river.

The men in the fields had seen the danger. They walked quickly back toward the fort. They were unarmed except for their hoes. As the farmers approached, their families poured out the small back gate.

Benjamin walked cautiously to address the deadly visitors. He made an effort to talk to them, but he did not speak Comanche, Spanish or the language of the hands. It was obvious the Indians were angry and in no mood to talk.

Benjamin knew there were only five men inside the fort counting himself. It was unlikely they could close the gates and mount any kind of defense before the Indians would be inside the fort. As he stalled for time, the main body of Indians rode out of the edge of the forest in a wide menacing line toward the fort. A quick glance gave an estimate of fifty or sixty Indians.

Attempting to signal to those still within the fort with his hands, he returned to the open main gate. Without turning his back on the Indians, he calmly called out in a loud voice that anyone left in the fort should run and the men in the fields should scatter.

His older brother, Silas, refused to give up so easily and grabbed a loaded musket. As soon as he appeared in the gate, an arrow took him in the shoulder. The advance guard of the Comanche attacked with a vengeance.

Silas tried to fire his musket with his uninjured arm, hitting nothing. War clubs and knives killed both men where they stood. The main body charged into the fort, except for a handful who pursued the men in the fields.

The massacre was quick and bloody. Five settlers lay dead, scalped and mutilated. Two women and three children were taken captive. The settlement's horses and mules were driven away with the Comanche. The attackers spent little time looking for those hiding in the thickets. They had scalps and horses, and did not have the patience to flush out the others. Gathering their captives and plunder, they rode off to the northwest.

———————

Seeing that the raiders had left, the devastated survivors slowly emerged from hiding. They returned to the fort where the gates were belatedly closed and barred. They buried their dead outside the walls under the protection of the rifles along the walls.

The Adamson family found that their youngest son, Parker, was missing. His brother, Kevin, had seen the Indians scoop him up on their departure. He had been named in honor of Benjamin Parker whose blood now stained the soil in front of the gate.

Several of the adults remembered that there was a militia company only fifteen miles away at Navasota Crossing. Kevin Adamson, and his older brother, Brian, offered to go for help. Before anyone had time to disagree with them, they were getting ready to go. A few horses had scattered into the brush and trees along the river. The Comanche had not made an effort to collect them. The boys caught two of the better horses and saddled up. Setting the horses into a lope, they headed down the river road to Navasota Crossing. Brian was seventeen and Kevin was thirteen. They were about to grow up fast.

2

May 19, 1836, Navasota Crossing, Leon County,
Republic of Texas

MY STEPSONS, LUCIUS
and Marcus King, had joined me in the shade of a live oak
tree to eat our lunch. The jerky and corn cakes tasted good,
chased down with the lukewarm water from our gourd
canteens. Since we had returned from San Jacinto we had
worked feverishly to get our neglected fields prepared
for planting. The corn was in the ground, but had not
sprouted yet. We had just started planting the cotton. The
wheat and oats would soon be ready to harvest.

We heard hoof beats coming at a run along the
river road from the north. Each of us grabbed our rifles
and checked the priming. Around a bend in the road we
saw a pair of lathered horses carrying white riders. We
didn't relax our grips on the rifles for fear of who might
be pursuing the riders.

"Whoa, boys! Pull in here." I waived my hat at the
riders.

The riders reined to a weary stop. The horses
heaved with each breath, covered with foamy sweat from
their forelocks to their tails.

"Are you Colonel Turner?" Brian asked as he slid from the saddle.

"Yes, son. Who are you and what's the hurry?"

"I'm Brian Adamson from Fort Parker. This here is my brother, Kevin."

He paused to catch his breath before continuing. "Comanche hit us this morning. Big war party. Killed five. Stole some women and kids, including my brother. Sent us for help."

Marcus brought water gourds for both of the boys. They nodded and drank deeply. They declined Lucius' offer of food.

"Marcus, unhitch your mule and ride like thunder to the settlement. Ring the bell to call the militia."

The clear baritone voice of the bell echoed along the river, through the settlement and over the fields. The tolling of the bell indicated to all who heard that there was an emergency. Farmers unhitched their draft animals and rode them home, leaving their implements in the fields. Women gathered their children inside and shuttered the windows and barred the doors. The more valuable livestock were quickly driven to the security of the stockade. The men and older boys grabbed their weapons and war bags and gathered at the gate of the fort. Shotguns and rifles appeared in gun ports from every building in the fort and the settlement as the women armed themselves.

Climbing up on the front porch of our house I addressed the gathering militia. "Men, we've got troubles close to home. The Comanche hit Fort Parker this morning; that's only fifteen miles up stream."

"There are two problems. First, we've gotta make sure the settlement is safe. Everybody has got to stay out of the fields until we're sure the Comanche are gone. Keep close to the fort, and keep your good animals there. Second, they need help at Fort Parker to try to recover the captives. I'm gonna take twenty men with me to see what we can do. All the rest of the militia is to remain here and protect our own folks."

We fed the exhausted boys and swapped their spent horses for fresh mounts. Richard Moore would be in command at the settlement in my absence. Nicholas Teel was to take five men and ride with all speed to warn Louisiana Landing of the danger. We did not know that they had already been raided. Nick was to join us at Fort Parker or somewhere along the trail with his detachment, unless danger closer to home required their presence.

I hand picked my company and set them gathering our supplies. Each man would carry two rifles, two saddle pistols, food, clothes and a bedroll. Chance, Cody, Tanner, Logan and Gray, my longtime friends, would ride with me. I could always count on them. Other men of the militia would round out our number. Three pack mules were loaded with oats, extra food and supplies. We took five extra horses with us in hopes of returning with the captives. By two in the afternoon we were riding hard for Fort Parker.

Fort Parker stood alert, bristling with weapons. Fresh graves were seen outside the walls. James Parker, the youngest surviving son of Elder John Parker, was in charge.

We entered the fort and talked briefly while the horses were watered. The women brought us corn bread and bacon while the men described the hostages and the war party.

It had been a mixed group of Comanche and Kiowa. They had left driving the stolen horses to the northwest. The Adamson boy was with them.

Brian and Kevin would not give up their efforts to rescue their brother. With their parents' approval, the folks of Fort Parker equipped them for the trip including guns and supplies.

"Mr. Adamson, I've got some young men with me who aren't much older than your boys, but they are battle tested veterans. I don't want to have to baby sit your boys."

"I understand, Colonel. They know how to handle a horse

and can ride all day without getting tired. They shoot as well as most of the men here. I think they'll hold up, but if they don't, you put both of them on the road home."

I reluctantly agreed. We rode until dark. The trail had been easy to follow. The Indians were making no effort to conceal their tracks. We made camp on an oak covered knoll surrounded by prairie. The timber would give us cover, and the open prairie would make an approaching enemy easy to see.

"Tanner, Gray, Logan, you boys tend the horses and mules. Lead them down to the spring at the bottom of the hills to water. Put hobbles on every last one of them and turn 'em out to graze for a while. Keep your eyes open. Chance, get some supper going. Use dry wood. We can't afford for the Comanche to see or smell smoke if we can help it."

Chance looked at Cody and grinned. "Colonel, could you help me wipe my nose? I plum forgot how to do it."

I turned on them with a flash of anger that immediately turned to a smile. "Guess I'm laying it on pretty thick. Cody, would you please see that the horses and mules are picketed good and tight and fed some oats. I would appreciate it so much." My voice dripped with sugar-coated sarcasm.

"Reckon I could do it as a special favor just for you, Colonel."

We finally gave way to a wave of laughter. I guess it relieved some of the day's stress. Those who knew us well just grinned. The others must have thought we had lost our minds.

Chance, the best tracker east of the Brazos, sat down to talk with me after supper. I had known Chance since he was a long-legged youth on our first trip to Texas in 1817. He had served as our guide and translator. He spoke English, Spanish, French, and several Indian languages fluently. He had been my strong right arm ever since. Cody and Nickolas Lane had been our muleskinners on that first trip. They all had fallen under the spell of Texas, just as I had. Like Chance, they were men I trusted with my life.

"Colonel, we're gettin' closer. The captives are probably slowing them down some, and herding the stolen horses and mules is holding them back. I don't see any way they can travel at night without losing the horses and mules. I think we ought to catch up to them pretty soon."

"I believe you're right. We're sure gonna have our hands full if we do catch them."

Cody had been sitting by the small fire listening to us talk. "With our extra rifles and pistols we can hold our own with a war band around our size. But the folks from Fort Parker thought there was fifty or sixty of them, and that's just the ones they saw."

"I'm hoping they want to get home with the horses more than anything. They're going to try to protect them. If I was a Comanche, I believe I'd drive the horse herd up front under guard, and leave a rear guard to handle the captives and fight off the militia."

"If they do divide up, I think we got a chance to fight 'em. I don't figure they'll all join up for fear of losin' the horses."

"I understand your idea, but what about the hostages?" Chance asked.

"To the Comanche they aren't worth as much as the horses. If they feel pressed too hard, I'm afraid they might just kill all the captives."

———

The next morning the horses were led to water and allowed to graze in the purple pre-dawn. Once the men were fed and the animals saddled, we resumed our pursuit of the Comanche raiders.

As we paused along a creek to eat a cold lunch and rest the horses, we saw five mounted white men with a pack mule following our trail. "Chance, take Cody with you and see what's goin' on."

Three of the men were their brothers-in-law, Blake, Tyler and Tanner Lane. All of them had married into the Applewhite family. Besides these three, two other men had joined them from Louisiana Landing. As usual, Tanner was the first one to speak. "Evenin', boys. Good to see y'all. We rode our butts plum off trying to catch you. Nick Teel told us about Fort Parker. We figure this is the same bunch that stole our horses."

"Big brother, even as ugly as you are, we're mighty glad to see y'all. We're gonna need every gun we get. What's this raid on your place?"

Blake spoke up. "Night before last about fifty or more Comanche riding with a few Kiowa raided our place. We all holed up and didn't nobody get hurt. They stole nearly every horse and mule on the place and burned the slaves' cabins and most of the barns. Our daddy-in-law is right worked up about it."

"I kinda got to feelin' like he had druther seen me and Blake and Tyler shot as to lose his good mules."

I was glad for the reinforcements and to know Nick had returned home with his men. I was still plenty worried about things at home.

_____

Chance scouted ahead of our party. He came galloping back in late afternoon. "Colonel, I saw two Comanche on a rise a couple of miles from here. They dang sure saw me, too. They know we're here now."

"I figure they knew we were here anyway. How close do you think we are to the main war band?"

"There's lots of tracks made by shod horses. The edges of the tracks are still sharp and fresh. The horse droppings aren't dried out and the birds haven't even been workin' on 'em yet. I think we're just a few miles away."

We pressed on with our rifles balanced across our laps. Just at dusk we found that the trail split. One set of tracks veered to the west, while the larger group continued northwest. The western trail had no tracks of shod horses, but the groups to the northwest had plenty.

We found a relatively safe place to make camp and set a double guard. The enemy was close. Chance, Cody and I sat down to talk about what to do next.

"Well, it seems obvious the horses went with the main war band to the northwest. There aren't enough of us to chase after both bunches. We're gonna go after the smaller band, because that is where I think the captives are."

"Colonel, the hostages are slowing them down. They want to get those horses home. I agree with you. The prisoners are gonna be with the smaller bunch. I think their job is to double back and attack us."

"I reckon you're both right. We oughta follow the main trail and make the smaller bunch come to us."

"Cody, you're as devious as an Apache. That's the plan."

———

By mid-morning, Chance returned at a hard gallop. "There's a war band of twenty or thirty Indians about two miles ahead. They've hidden themselves behind a ridge where they can ambush us on the trail. They've got hostages with them. Let's give them a little surprise."

When we were within half a mile of the anticipated ambush, we left the trail and crossed behind the same ridge that was hiding our foes. We kept the horses at a fast walk until we were within a quarter mile of the last place Chance had seen the Indians.

"Assemble in two rows across, move out at a lope."

Our luck had held. The Comanche had not expected us from this direction. They quickly turned their horses to counter our charge with their lances and bows. We were now within a hundred yards of them.

"Halt! Front rank, fire!"

Fourteen rifles spoke almost as one, and four Indians fell to the ground dead or wounded. The Comanche kept coming hard and now were within extreme bow range.

"Second rank, fire!"

Another fourteen rifles barked. Half a dozen Comanche fell as arrows began to land among us.

"Company, engage!"

The Comanche were now all among us. Our .69 caliber saddle

pistols were deadly at close range. Eight more Indians died. A man from home was struck down by a war club. He would never see another sunrise. As we fired our second pistols, six more Comanche fell. The remainder fled the ravine and disappeared over the crest of the ridge.

We had killed or wounded twenty-four of their number. We had lost one man, and two horses had arrow wounds.

In the commotion of the initial attack, three hostages had managed to jerk free from the rawhide thongs around their necks and kick their horses into a gallop straight for us. There were other hostages still with the Comanche.

We wheeled our horses and headed to friendlier country. Logan Morgan and Gray tied the dead man on his skittish horse and raced after us.

Behind us we could see some of the wounded crawling to safety. As we drew farther away, mounted Indians swept down and carried away the dead and wounded. Comanche would rarely leave a dead comrade behind if they had a choice.

In the aftermath, we were able to claim five Indian horses and three hostages, Parker Adamson among them. Our other two rescued hostages were Mexican boys of twelve or thirteen years old. They had been taken captive a few months before when the Comanche had raided deep into Mexico. Both of them had seen all the rest of their families killed at the hands of the Comanche. They spoke no English, but most of us spoke good Spanish. They related their ordeal to us. One was a little taller and wiry. His name was Aaron Chavez from somewhere in Coahuila. The other was stocky built and quieter. His name was Angelo Lucio from the mountains of Chihuahua. They were to have been sold as slaves to the Comancheros. They were mighty glad to have gotten away.

We had failed to free the other captives. Rachel Plummer and her son remained prisoners, as did John Richard Parker and his sister, Cynthia Ann. The Comanche had suffered a few casualties, but returned home with many horses, mules and a few scalps. For them, the raid of May 1836 had been a huge success.

3

September 1836, Navasota Crossing, Leon County, Republic of Texas

THE TIME HAD COME for Texas to get better organized as a Republic. The provisional government was to be replaced by elected officials and a legislature. Texas was divided into twenty-three counties. There would be fourteen senatorial districts and twenty-nine representative districts. Each county was to elect a sheriff, a constable, and a justice of the peace.

Our friend, Sam Houston, was elected president by a landslide. Mirabeau B. Lamar was elected vice-president. The two disliked each other to an extreme degree, perhaps rising to the level of hatred. The beloved Stephen Austin was appointed Secretary of State.

I was elected justice of the peace for Leon County. Richard Moore was chosen sheriff, and Nick Lane was to be constable. Our offices became official October 3, 1836.

The Congress of the Republic of Texas met at Columbia. It presided over a new nation of approximately thirty thousand Anglo settlers, five thousand slaves, three thousand Mexicans and fifteen thousand settled Indians. There was no way to estimate the population of the Plains Indians or the Apache. They still controlled most of the

Republic west of the Colorado River. Of the white settlers, seventy five percent had been born in the southern United States, and most were of English, Scots, or Irish heritage.

The Republic awarded each head of a family a league and a labor of land, or just over four thousand six hundred acres. Single men received a third as much, or over fifteen hundred acres.

Rather than issue specific tracts of land, the Republic issued scrip which could be redeemed for a specified number of acres. The scrip could be used to claim that number of acres from the public domain at the General Land Office. Because it was backed with land, the scrip was traded like cash and widely accepted. Its value was negotiable between the buyer and seller of the scrip depending on supply and demand. There was an almost limitless supply of land in Texas, and an almost equal appetite for it. Every one wanted land. The land scrip became in effect the earliest "money" of the Republic of Texas.

———

The fall of 1836 was the first time most Texans had experienced anything more serious than a little horse stealing from our friends the Caddo and their relatives, the Wichita. The Cherokee and Kickapoo pressured the Caddo and Wichita from the northeast, while the Comanche made life nearly impossible in the northwest.

The Texan settlers to the south now presented themselves as the easiest of targets for these previously peaceful tribes. The Wichita raided from their homelands in north central Texas between the upper Brazos and the Red River. The Caddo raided from the headwaters of the Trinity River. The area between the Trinity and the Brazos was the site of heavy raiding in 1836. There was no regular army stationed within hundreds of miles and only militia units to interfere with Indian raids.

The largest settlement in this large area was Navasota Crossing. We stood like a bull's eye in the middle of their raiding grounds. I was still in command of the militia in the entire area.

The early raids had been mostly against isolated cabins and small undefended settlements. Our long-term allies, the Tonkawa, remained true friends and helped the Texans against their Indian enemies.

In the fall days between corn harvest and cotton picking we received news that the Wichita and Caddo had made common cause and were camped on the headwaters of the Navasota River preparing for a massive strike. Their camp was only a few miles from Fort Parker.

I called Chance, the Teel bothers, Richard Moore and Joe Morgan to my cabin. I explained the situation. "Men, there is no time to waste. We must hit the Indians before they launch their raid. Assemble the militia. Move all the better livestock inside the stockade. Get the settlers from the farthest cabins here until this is over. Richard, as County Sheriff, I'm leaving you in charge here. Chance, pick twenty men to leave behind, and everyone else goes with us. Nick, get word to Captain Rob at Louisiana Landing to get as many men as he can spare to Fort Parker on the third of November. Cody, get our horses and supplies ready to go."

In two days we set out up the river road along the Navasota to Fort Parker. The Tonkawa scouts confirmed the Indians had not yet broken camp. We brought fully a hundred men and a dozen scouts for our pre-emptive strike. Another forty men arrived from Louisiana Landing. David Adamson, his three sons, and seven other men from Fort Parker joined us.

We left our horses inside the six acre enclosure of the fort. We would approach the camp on foot, using the thick brush and timber to screen our approach. The Tonkawa went ahead of us to make sure we didn't wander into trouble. In the event things did not go well, we would fall back to the fort.

The Tonkawa reported that better than two hundred Wichita and Caddo were assembled there for feasting and dancing. They had not brought their women and children. The only guards set appeared to be the few men watching the horse herd. Their large number seemed to have made them complacent.

We assembled the men in a broad semi-circle four ranks deep southwest of the camp. The setting sun was behind us and would be in the faces of our enemies. The Tonkawa silently approached the camp from the southeast. Without a sound, they killed the few braves guarding the horses. Mounting the slain guards' horses, they stampeded the horse herd through the middle of the camp and directly toward us.

The enraged Indians grabbed their weapons and charged after the fleeing Tonkawa. We lay flat on the ground as the horses jumped over and around us. When the approaching enemy was at fifty yards we opened volley fire by rank. We each carried two rifles, so we were able to fire eight volleys in rapid succession into the surprised Indians.

As the last shot was fired, we stood and charged into the confused survivors. We clubbed them with our empty rifles yelling like demons from hell. We used our tomahawks, knives and pistols to deadly effect.

A Wichita brave turned to fight Cody with a stone war club. Cody sidestepped the blow and plunged his knife under the warrior's ribs.

Logan faced a large Caddo who fought with a tomahawk and knife. A load of buckshot from Logan's .69 caliber pistol ended the fight before it had begun.

Tanner and Gray stayed close to Logan as they always did. A Wichita lunged at Tanner with a heavy war club striking a glancing blow across his right shoulder, breaking his collar bone.

Gray seized the moment when the Wichita had his arm extended and slashed down with his steel tomahawk, severing the man's arm at the elbow. A second blow to the head finished him.

Another Indian attacked the injured Tanner as he lay on the ground. Tanner used his left arm to raise and fire his pistol, shooting his enemy full in the chest.

Blake Lane used the barrel of his empty rifle to split the head of a persistent Caddo. Chance was attacked by a Wichita swinging a war club. He used his tomahawk to jerk the club to the side and plunge his knife deep in the man's belly with his left hand.

The Tonkawa had ridden back into the melee. They jumped off their horses and attacked with a bloody fury.

The last of the Indians threw down their weapons; only thirty-two had survived. One of the men from Louisiana Landing had been killed in the fight. Tanner had a broken collar bone. Another man had his leg broken when the stampeding horses had landed on him. We were able to patch them up enough to travel.

There were no surviving leaders left among them with whom to negotiate. Many of the militia wanted to execute them. We had all suffered at the hands of various Indians in the past. Enough blood had been shed. I would not allow them to hurt our captives. After we made sure there were no hidden weapons, we marched them to Fort Parker. We locked them in one of the block houses, tied hand and foot, and set a heavy guard. We passed jerky and water around to them and left them for the night.

We were famished. The good women of Fort Parker had prepared a big meal of beans and corn bread for our supper. It was just what we needed. We fell into exhausted sleep inside the stockade.

The next morning, I sent Chance and ten men to escort the twenty surviving unarmed and dismounted Wichita away to the northwest. A day's walk away from the fort he was to release them. Cody and half a dozen men would escort the surviving twelve Caddo to the northeast. Although scattered groups of Wichita and Caddo would join other Indians in raids against Texans, the current threat was ended.

_____

The cotton yielded only an average crop. Once it was picked, Lucius, Cody and Nick rafted the bales down river. They met Captain Rob with the *Brazos Belle* at Groce's Plantation. Rob gave them the news that Stephen Austin had died of pneumonia a few days earlier. The "Father of Texas" was no more.

4

Spring, 1837, Navasota Crossing, Leon County,
Republic of Texas

THE END OF THE FIGHT-
ing with Mexico had seen a return of immigrants to Texas.
They flowed down the Camino Real, the main overland
route from the United States to the opportunities of Texas.
Settlers came in wagons, on horseback, pushing hand
carts or on foot. They all came with hopes for a better life
and a new start.

A settlement was growing where the Camino
Real crossed the Trinity River, only thirty miles to our
east. There was talk of steamboat service extending from
the coast to north Texas as the need developed.

To the south, a small village was growing where
the Navasota met the Brazos. To the north, there were
still only isolated farms. To the west, a tiny community
was springing up on the Camino Real about half way to
Louisiana Landing.

Tanner Lane was hauling a load of freight to the
new settlement on the Trinity River when he pulled up in
front of the house. "Howdy, Colonel. You ain't dead yet?"

"Good to see you, too, jug head. Guess you're huntin' free food and lodging as usual?"

"I reckon so. I even brought you a newspaper from San Felipe that ain't even a week old. You be nice and I'll just let you keep it."

He handed me a copy of the Texas Gazette. It held good news for Texas. On March 3, 1837, after resolutions by the Congress of the United States, President James K. Polk had signed documents recognizing the Republic of Texas. Alcee LaBranche was sent to Columbia as the Ambassador to Texas.

"Well, I guess that makes Texas a real country now that the United States says we are. That's about all we got out of the deal. Let's get your mules tended to. Supper won't be long. I just hope we can fill you up!"

"Miss Nancy's cooking is always fillin' and always good. Say, I want to tell you a whopper of a true story."

"You wouldn't know a true story if it bit you on the nose, but I'm listenin'."

"That ol' sour puss Felix Huston was made commander of the army by the provisional government. He had about two thousand men at San Antonio thinkin' he might just invade Mexico. When Sam Houston got elected President, he wanted to clip that ol' rooster's spurs, so he appointed Albert Sydney Johnston as commander. When he went down to relieve Huston of command, he refused and got so mad he challenged Johnston to a duel. They stepped outside and shot at each other and both missed. They did it again and again. On the sixth try, Huston finally shot Johnston in the hip. It's a wonder we ever beat Mexico with officers that shoot like that!"

"Six times? What finally happened?"

"Since Huston wouldn't quit the army, ol' Sam invited him to a dinner in his honor in Columbia. While he was there, Sam Houston sent all the soldiers home except six hundred men. Huston wouldn't leave the army, so it left him."

That night after supper, Tanner sat with Nancy and me in the parlor as I finished reading the Gazette. "Looks like the Republic finally got around to setting some taxes. It doesn't look too bad. There's a one percent tax on wheat and flour you don't grow yourself, a poll tax to vote, plus a business tax, license fee and a small tonnage tax on imports. There are going to be small fees to register land claims, but it is this last tax I'm worried about?"

"What's that, dear?"

"A luxury tax on imported china, crystal, silverware, wine, and such like. I sure hope we can afford to keep up our standard of living!"

We all enjoyed a good laugh as there wasn't anything remotely luxurious for hundreds of miles in any direction. That was one tax we wouldn't have to worry about paying.

"I forgot to tell you the most important thing. My wife, Emily, had a baby boy. We named him Charles."

"We had heard about it. Congratulations! I hope Emily has recovered and the baby is well." Nancy added.

"What are you hauling this far to the east, anyway?"

"My daddy-in-law, Mister Applewhite, has me delivering the makings of a cotton gin with all the belts, rollers and gears, plus stones for using it to grind grain, too. There is even a set of rollers for pressing ribbon cane. He put me up in his best wagon with his four heaviest mules."

"I saw your rig. You'll be traveling in fine style unless the road is muddy. There are some places east of here that just don't have a bottom when it's been raining."

"Oh, Colonel, I've been driving in the mud since I was five years old. I never got stuck that I couldn't get out of it."

As he spoke, a rumble of thunder shook the house. A slow gentle rain started that continued all night.

The next morning, Tanner ate enough breakfast for three men. Nancy gave him biscuits and bacon for his lunch. He thanked us and flipped the reins to get his wagon moving.

In about an hour, Tanner was back riding one of his mules.

Both the rider and the mule were covered in sticky red mud.

"Colonel, I got a little problem. The wagon is bogged down in the mud and I can't get it out. Would you mind helping me?"

"Been driving in the mud since you were five, huh? Well, I guess I'll help you anyway."

We harnessed my two best draft mules. I rode one and led one and Tanner rode the other. When I saw the wagon, I knew we were in a mess. It was sunk to the hubs on all four wheels. We put Tanner's mule back in her place and added my two up front. Tanner laid into the mules with most ungentlemanly language, but the combined strength of all six mules could not budge the wagon.

"Well, Tanner, you scorched their hair a little with the cussin' you gave 'em, but you're still stuck. Let's unload some of the cargo."

We unloaded everything that the two of us could move, but much of it was too heavy. We tried again. All six pulled and strained with a will, but the wagon only moved a few inches.

"Let's ride back and get some more help." Tanner didn't have much to say.

I spotted Tanner Moore, Logan and Gray loafing on the front porch of the store. They had come with the first families in 1821. "You boys are just what we need. Strong backs and weak minds."

We borrowed four more good mules from Marcus and Lucius. The boys seemed glad to have something to do.

When we arrived, we hitched the extra mules to the wagon. We had ten strong mules hitched together. The driving reins wouldn't reach beyond the third pair, so each of the boys and Tanner took a mule by the headstall and I climbed into the wagon box.

"Hup, mules! Hup! Pull, you sorry outfits! Pull!"

The whip cracked and the mules pulled. The wagon rolled forward only to slide back again. We tried again with the same results.

"Well, boys, let's unload the wagon."

The five of us were able to unload the cane press, the grain mill, the heavy leather belts and gears, but we couldn't budge the huge gin rollers.

We returned our attention to the wagon. Tanner got a shovel and dug in front of the wheels as best he could. The heavy red clay and mud stubbornly clung to the wheels and his shovel. This time the ten draft mules were able to free the wheels from the sucking red mud. I drove the wagon to where the road was solid.

We unhitched all but the two wheel mules that were hitched right next to the wagon. Tanner cautiously backed the wagon to the freight on the road. We reloaded the wagon and hitched the two lead mules to their rightful position. Once the wagon was reloaded, Tanner backed the wagon a little further so that when he hit the soft spot in the road there would be enough speed to clear the mud. With a loud oath and a fearful crack of the whip, the wagon lurched forward and was almost immediately picking up speed. When the four mules hit the mud, he cracked the whip again and the wagon cleared the soft spot without a problem. Tanner didn't slow down, but kept the mules trotting ahead. He shouted his thanks and waved as the muddy wagon rolled down the road.

An innovation in firearms had occurred. Rather than a flint and powder pan, guns could be fired with a percussion cap. This would solve the problems of wind blowing the powder out of the pan or wet weather causing a misfire. There was no worry about a broken flint. The conversion from a flintlock to a percussion cap weapon was relatively simple for a competent gunsmith like Richard Moore or his son, Tanner. The hammer was replaced to strike a cap, and the flash pan was replaced with a steel nipple to accept a cap. The copper percussion caps were filled with a compound that exploded with the impact of the hammer. There was less lag time from the time the trigger was pulled until the powder fired. The caps were inexpensive and easy to obtain. Richard and Tanner stayed busy converting flintlocks into percussion cap guns. I had all of my guns changed as soon as possible.

Sam Houston moved the capital to the new town named in his honor on the banks of Buffalo Bayou. The move was not popular with his political opponents.

Word arrived from the coast that the banking system in the United States was in tatters. Banks were failing each day. Merchants would only accept coin for sales, and everyone was hording their coins. Commerce came to a virtual standstill. People resorted to the centuries old system of barter. This was nothing new on the frontier. Barter was a way of life. However, it strongly affected the willingness to spend any type of coin unless absolutely necessary. Land scrip appreciated in value. It was readily accepted in trade. In times of financial turmoil, land was almost always a safe investment.

The Republic of Texas issued scrip redeemable in public land as payment to those who had fought in the War for Independence redeemable in public land. Those who had served any length of time received scrip equal to a half section of land, or three hundred and twenty acres. Those who had served for the duration of the war received an additional three hundred and twenty acres. Finally, those who had fought at San Jacinto received scrip for another half section. Most of us at Navasota Crossing would receive scrip equal to nine hundred and sixty acres.

The Republic also issued half a million dollars in bearer bonds at twelve percent payable in coin in one year. These were widely accepted and circulated. The economy of Texas suffered, but did not collapse.

_____

I received a letter from my older brother, James, in South Carolina.

Dear Aaron,

We are well here. All of my children are married now, and I have three grandchildren. My sons have taken up farming here. We still raise a little tobacco and plenty of corn and farm crops. We stopped growing indigo several years ago. It seems the German's have invented a blue dye that costs only a fraction of the cost of indigo. To be honest, I do not miss it.

I hope you and Nancy and the children are well. I have enjoyed your occasional letters.

I am writing to let you know that the financial panic in the United States has resulted in the demise of Turner Shipping and Trade. All of the shares are now worthless. Let us hope for better days ahead.
Your brother,

James

———————

A consequence of the financial panic in the United States was the collapse of the cotton market. There was little cash and no credit for the mills to buy cotton. The price dropped to two cents a pound. It was not enough to cover the cost of growing, picking, ginning, baling and shipping it to market. That fall, we picked, ginned and baled our cotton, but did not send it to the coast. We decided to store it until the price improved. We needed a cotton warehouse.

We raised a foundation a foot above the ground to keep the bales dry and off the ground if there were heavy rains. The sides were left open for ventilation, but the roof had four foot eaves all the way around. We determined not to plant any more cotton until we could see profit in doing it.

5

Spring, 1838, Navasota Crossing, Leon County, Republic of Texas

THE FINANCIAL PANIC in the United States worked the greatest hardship on the poor. They poured in a sad stream down the Camino Real to escape creditors and start a new life in Texas.

Many of these new settlers found the forests and woodlands of east Texas similar to their former homes. They filed claims for land in an area that had previously received scant attention between the Sabine and Trinity Rivers. They also settled in the northeast part of the Republic between the Red River and the upper reaches of the Trinity.

Unfortunately, much of that land had become home to the Cherokee, Delaware, Shawnee and Kickapoo who had moved into the area in the previous twenty years displacing the original Caddo Indians. Conflicts were inevitable.

The more peaceful Caddo had been no match for the more warlike tribes. They had simply given up their ancestral homes and moved west. But their migration had already caused problems with white settlers and their eventual defeat. They had mostly relocated to Indian Territory, even though scattered pockets remained.

The eastern tribes had obtained their new lands through conquest of the Caddo, and they were ready to fight like cougars to keep them from the hands of the new settlers. When the conflict came, it would be major.

———————

Not all the new settlers stayed in east Texas. Many pushed on to the unclaimed lands beyond the Colorado, and some stayed in our area. From among the new settlers' daughters, Tanner Moore, Logan Morgan and Gray Jamison all chose brides. They had been inseparable friends for more than fifteen years. It came as no surprise when they asked me to perform a triple wedding.

Tanner had become an accomplished gunsmith under his father's guidance. His bride was a beautiful girl from Mississippi named Mary Taylor. She had bright flashing eyes, and a captivating smile. He filed a land claim and built a tidy cabin east of the settlement. Other than a large garden plot, all of his land was intended for grazing.

Logan had learned the trade of a carpenter from his father. He could build anything from wood with remarkable skill. A beautiful dark haired young woman from Alabama named Brooke had caught his eye. He filed a claim next to Tanner's and built a very nice home of sawn lumber with glass windows and a tile roof. Twenty acres of his claim was intended for a garden and growing corn, while the rest was good pasture.

Gray was working as a clerk for one of the local lawyers and reading the law in preparation for establishing his own practice. His heart had been won by a young woman with a sparkling smile and bubbly personality named Abigail from Arkansas. He filed a claim joining both Tanner and Logan on the south. He built his house near Logan's on the road. The land was mostly good pasture bordering woodlands.

The wedding was the social event of the spring of 1838. The brides quickly became close friends. The "boys," as I usually called them, began to put together a herd of good cattle and built a rail fence around the perimeter of their combined property. The partnership, like the friendship, would endure for many years.

———————

I didn't plant any cotton that year. We ran a harrow over the old cotton rows and sowed black-eyed peas into the freshened soil. The peas would be good to eat fresh or dried for later use. They could also be made good livestock feed.

I grew more corn than usual and a little extra ribbon cane for syrup. The excess should be easy to barter.

At the store I took jerky and cow hides in trade. I could barter those for sugar, coffee, cloth, nails, hardware and house goods.

Our own production kept the shelves stocked with corn meal, as well as sacked corn, oats and black-eyed peas for feed. I took in cured bacon, lard, jerky, shelled pecans, honey, eggs and butter which I resold in the store. Travelers always seemed to need these things as they passed through. Sometimes there was a little surplus flour to sell, but seldom in amounts of more than one to five pounds. I traded for locally made inexpensive tallow candles and the more expensive beeswax candles.

The brick works sold bricks, roofing tile and pottery. The tannery's finished hides went to the local harness maker and to Mr. Black, the cobbler, for boots and brogans. Both men did good work and their products were in demand. The other tradesmen were busy and managed to keep their families fed by bartering, accepting land scrip and the occasional transaction in coin. Navasota Landing now had a full-time barber who stayed busy with shaves and haircuts.

There was now a small distillery operating north of us on Boggy Creek. They bought locally grown corn, locally made oak barrels and pottery jugs. Selling corn by the gallon made more money than selling it by the bushel. They never seemed to have a problem selling all of their production.

Our community had grown from a frontier fort to an

established center of commerce. In spite of the recent war with Mexico, on-going Indian troubles and a shaky larger economy, Navasota Landing survived and prospered.

———————

Mexico had reneged on the Treaty of Velasco. They claimed that Santa Anna had no authority to negotiate a treaty on behalf of Mexico. They considered Texas a Mexican province in rebellion. Efforts never ceased to undermine the fragile young Republic. General Filisola commanded an army of roughly four thousand Mexican infantry and cavalry in Matamoras, ready to sweep into Texas at any time.

Filisola dispatched a Mexican agent, Vicente Cordova, to spread seeds of hatred among the Tejanos and Indians of Texas, especially around Nacogdoches. In July, Cordova met with Duwali, High Chief of the Cherokee, and chiefs of the Kickapoo, Shawnee and Delaware. He convinced them that Mexico would give them secure titles to their lands if they would drive the Texans beyond the Brazos. It was Mexico's intention that, while the Indians kept the Texans busy in the northeast, the Mexicans would push up from the southwest. Cordova had been given money to buy guns, horses and tobacco to encourage the Indians to join his plan. By August, 1838, Cordova had assembled a combined group of six hundred Indians of various tribes and Tejanos at a camp on the Angelina River north of Nacogdoches. From this central point, they began large scale successful raids to drive out the settlers, burn their cabins, and steal their livestock.

Secretary of War Thomas J. Rusk called out the militia to address this problem. Among other groups, the militia at Louisiana Landing and Navasota Crossing were called to duty. Although I was the lieutenant colonel in charge of the militia in northeast Texas, I was out ranked by numerous colonels and generals of the Republic of Texas, not to mention the Secretary of War himself. My command was basically limited to my own militia and that under Captain Rob. There were no other active militia units in my district.

However, as district commander I was included in the war councils and I was consulted on some issues. Chance was still a major but was a significant participant in the process. His familiarity with the native languages and his ability as a tracker made him invaluable to the whole campaign.

The militias were joined by regular troops. The entire Texan force was over three hundred well-armed, well-supplied men.

I was part of an advance group sent to parlay with the assembled chiefs. No Tejanos were to be seen. Cordova had vanished like a mist into the forest. The chiefs denied that they even knew him. President Houston's emissary explained that steps would be taken to secure their land claims and to stabilize their vulnerable position. The various tribes agreed to disperse and to return in peace to their own villages. I had a feeling this would not be the last we heard of the matter.

We returned home to finish up our crops. The corn was hardly in the cribs before the Indians resumed their raiding.

Aaron Chavez and Angelo Lucio had no families to which they could return. Nancy and I took them in to our home. They worked hard in the fields and with the livestock. Both were accomplished riders. Aaron was an talented musician and could play any number of stringed instruments, especially the guitar. Angelo was one of the best story tellers any of us remembered. He would entertain anyone who wanted to listen. During their stay with the Comanche they had learned the difficult language, as well as the language of the hands. Besides their native Spanish, they quickly became fluent in English as well. They were old enough now that they rode with the militia. Their hatred of the Comanche easily transferred to whatever tribe we would fight. And they fought with a deadly passion, full of vengeance.

On September 8, 1838, a large war party attacked a surveying crew on Battle Creek, north of Nacogdoches. Seventeen men were killed and five wounded.

On October 5, 1838, a mixed band of Cherokee Indians and Tejanos fell on the small settlement belonging to the Killough family. Eighteen victims were found dead. Several others were dragged away into the forest and never seen again. There were only seven people who survived by hiding in a cane brake.

Secretary Rusk again assembled a force to intervene. The feeling was we were going to do what should have been done the first time. We unfurled the Lone star flag and rode to the Neches River. A large body of Indians was camped at a Kickapoo village in a horseshoe bend of Kickapoo Creek, a half mile upstream from the Neches.

As our scouts approached, they could see the Indians evacuating the camp and heading off into the thickly forested hills north of the village. When the main body arrived, we found the village abandoned. Our scouts found no signs of the Indians in the area. Secretary Rusk ordered us to set up camp for the night in the village, with one third of the men on guard duty at any given time.

"Secretary Rusk?"

"What is it Colonel Turner?"

"Major Chance and I both feel that the Indian withdrawal from the village is a trap, sir. I suggest we find a more defensible campsite."

"Nonsense. They fled before a superior force. We have water and shelter here. Our scouts found no signs of them in the area."

"That's just it, sir. If they were fleeing a superior force, I believe we would have found sign that they had left. I still think it's an ambush, sir."

"Well, Colonel Turner, when you are Secretary of War, you can make the decisions. Until then, you will follow orders."

I bristled at the tone of his remarks. Chance put his hand on my arm and shook his head.

"It's not worth it. He's got his mind made up. No point in confusing him with the facts."

During the long, tense night, mosquitoes hung in living clouds around us. Even Chance's smelly miracle salve did not keep them away. The air was heavy with moisture. Some of Cordova's men tossed burning torches into the leaf thatch on the forest floor around the village. The damp air kept it from burning well, but it smoldered all night. The acrid smell of smoke hung over the camp as a blanket, adding to our discomfort. Not a night bird sang to lighten our gloom, but the forest itself whispered a warning that went unheeded.

———————

The Kickapoo, Cherokee, Tejanos and Mexicans attacked at dawn. They came screaming from the forest like demons straight from hell. The attackers pressed our position hard from the north, while skirmishers on the flanks kept us penned down.

Rusk personally led a charge out of the Kickapoo Village directly into the thickest concentration of the enemy. He might have lacked judgment, but he was not lacking in courage. He sent smaller detachments to sweep the flanks and root out the skirmishers.

My men were assigned to the main counter attack on the north. Rob, Chance and I rallied the men forward.

Tanner Lane barely escaped the blast of a Mexican escopeta. The Tejano lunged forward with a bayonet which snagged in the heavy underbrush. Before the man could react, Tanner split his head with the butt of his rifle.

The enemy started to fall back under the pressure of our advance. A Kickapoo warrior sprang from the thick brush directly at Gray. He swung a huge heavy war club barely missing Gray's face. The momentum of the heavy club briefly exposed his right shoulder and back. Like a flash of lightning, Gray struck with his tomahawk. The razor sharp blade caught him in the neck, almost decapitating the Kickapoo.

A large light skinned Cherokee appeared from behind a tree

with his bow raised at Logan. Before he could aim the arrow, Logan shot him in the face with his saddle pistol.

Enraged, Aaron Chavez and Angelo Lucio fell on the retreating Indians with pistols, knives and tomahawks with a deadly vengeance. Their faces and clothes were splattered with blood and gore.

The enemy skirmishers on the flanks fell back quickly from the unexpectedly fierce counter attack. When the main body broke and ran, both flanks disintegrated and the Battle of Kickapoo Village was over.

A dozen horses had been injured from arrows shot into the village. Thirteen Texans had been wounded but none had been killed. We made no effort to count the Indian losses, but estimated them somewhere over twenty.

I saw Chavez and Lucio as they washed their hands and faces at the camp. Aaron had a bloody scalp tucked in his belt. Angelo had two. Their anger for the slaughter of their families by the Comanche ran deep within them. This would end the Indian troubles for a while, but with the agitations of Cordova, the troubles would return. The Lone Star flag would soon be unfurled in anger again.

6

January, 1839, Navasota Crossing, Leon County,
Republic of Texas

HARD MONEY WAS STILL
in very short supply in Texas. Chance approached me
with an idea.

"Colonel, we've pretty well caught all the wild
horses in this area. But there are still lots of them for
the taking to the west between the Red River and the
upper Brazos. Let's put together a group to catch wild
horses. Once they're green broke, we can drive them to
Natchitoches to sell or trade. I think my daddy would be
able to put together some good trades, and maybe even a
little silver for them."

"Well, the Comanche ought to be snugged down
in the canyons on the edge of the plains for the winter.
Maybe if we don't get too close to them we won't stir up
a fight. There's still some Wichita up there that ain't too
friendly."

"I thought about that. We could find their winter
camp and trade them some salt, tobacco, cloth and
blankets for their permission to hunt there."

"Cody, Nick, what do ya' think?"

Nick had been nodding in agreement. "Heck,

Colonel, I need to get away from Kassie and the kids anyway. They're driving me crazy."

"There ain't gonna be no Karankawa up there, so I guess I'm in on the deal."

"Alright, I want to check with Nancy. If she is alright with the idea, you can deal me in, too."

That night after supper as Nancy and I sat by the fire in the front room, I opened the topic. "Some of the other men are planning a trip to gather wild horses on the upper Brazos. I kinda thought I'd go with them if you don't care."

Nancy put down the wool she was carding. "Are Marcus and Lucius going, or staying here with their families?"

"You know those two are a lot more about farming than catching wild horses in Indian country. I hadn't planned on even asking them."

"Same deal as always. I don't care if you go, as long as you promise to come back."

"The other men were rolling their eyes and teasing me because I wanted to talk to you first. I don't think they know what a real good woman I got." A smile and a kiss sealed the deal.

We loaded a sturdy wagon with food, supplies and trade goods. We also brought arm loads of heavy leather halters with long heavyweight lead ropes. I chose my four best mules to pull the wagon.

The idea of the horse expedition had proven popular. Cody, Nick and Chance were leaving their families to go. Tanner Lane had ridden over from Louisiana Landing to join us. Gray, Logan and Tanner Moore had said good bye to their brides for some adventure. Gray and Tanner had their wives move in with Richard Moore's family inside the fort. Logan's wife moved in with his parents at the fort. Aaron Chavez and Angelo Lucio begged to go. I agreed, as extra men with rifles might prove useful.

———

Frost sparkled on the windows and cabin roofs as we bid our families good bye. The horses' breath steamed in the crisp morning air making them look like fire-breathing dragons as they pawed and pranced, anxious to be off.

I drove the wagon with Charlie, my favorite bay gelding tied behind the tail gate. I was glad the wagon had good springs and a spring seat. My back didn't handle pot holes as well as it did when I was younger. Besides a heavy wool coat, I had a well tanned buffalo robe wrapped around me. The wagon tarp was up on the bows and provided some shelter from the wind. The riders strung out behind the wagon. Chance took his customary position scouting ahead of the wagon a hundred yards or so.

We followed the wagon trail along the east bank of the Navasota until we reached Fort Parker. We had made fifteen miles so far, a good start. We stopped to spend the night at the fort, as it was too late in the day to make much more progress. It felt good to be out of the cold and eat a hot meal. After supper, David Adamson asked if his three sons could join us.

"David, I know those older two can handle themselves without a baby sitter. What about the little one?"

"That's Parker, the one you rescued. He isn't so little since the last time you saw him. He is as big as his brothers, and he can handle a horse or gun as well as either of them."

I looked up to see him talking to Chavez and Lucio with whom he had shared a few days of captivity. "Well, I don't care if you don't. I don't have time to be wiping his nose, so his brothers are going to have to take care of him."

"Once you spend a little time with Parker, you'll see he can take care of himself and them, too."

_____

We camped the next night on the same knoll where we had stayed after the Fort Parker raid. Chance had scouted far ahead of us and found the Wichita winter encampment.

In the morning Chance, Chavez, Lucio and I rode out to talk with the Wichita about capturing horses. The horses were loaded with gifts to make our request a little more likely to succeed. Nick was in charge in my absence.

We approached within sight of the village and stopped with our rifles extended above our heads. A dozen Wichita grabbed their weapons and sprang onto their horses staked by their lodges. In less than a minute they had us surrounded.

My throat tightened as my pulse quickened. I only spoke a little of any of the Wichita languages, but Chance was fluent. He was our spokesman.

"We come in peace. We want to smoke with you, to talk, to bring you gifts."

A powerful brave in his mid-twenties spoke. "I am Many Coups. On my scalp pole hang the hair of many white men, Mexicans, Tonkawa, and Comanche. I will take you to Finds the Buffalo. If you do not come in peace, I will add your scalps to the others. Do you understand?"

We all nodded some measure of understanding. We were escorted to the lodge of Finds the Buffalo. A warrior of heavy build stood with his arms crossed in front of his lodge.

He turned to address me in good English. "I speak English, Spanish and Wichita. What tongue do you prefer?"

"Your English is good. I speak English and Spanish, but only a little Wichita. My scout speaks your tongue well. It will be as you wish."

"Leave your horse here with the two boys to make sure we do not steal from you." He turned and smiled. "We are good at stealing from white men."

Chance and I stooped to enter the winter lodge. It was not a towering teepee of the Comanche. It was shorter and less decorated. The covering was of buffalo skins with several cow hides; some of which had brands. It was tidy, but cramped and smoky. The dozen braves who had escorted us into the village stood guard around the lodge.

"Who are you and why do you disturb my winter camp? The Wichita have suffered much at the hands of your people."

"I am Aaron Turner from a settlement on the Navasota River. I know of the bad blood between the Wichita and the whites. It was not always so. I had many friends among your people. My people have seen a hard winter. We have come to catch wild horses that we may trade them for food and things we need for our people."

"Why should I let you do this?"

"There are many wild horses on your hunting grounds, like the birds of the air. We will only take a few of them. We will only kill enough other animals for our own food. We have brought you gifts if you will let us catch horses and keep the peace with us while we are here."

"I will think on it. What gifts have you brought?"

"Chavez, bring in the gifts. Lucio, stay with the horses."

Aaron brought in three bolts of good sturdy wool cloth in blue, dark green and red. He returned with five cloth bags of salt and five of tobacco. He made a final trip and carried in a dozen good wool blankets. I then sent Aaron back outside."

"We will smoke while I think." He reached for one of the tobacco pouches and thoughtfully filled his pipe. He lit it with a burning taper from the fire. He blew smoke to the earth, the sky, and to the four sacred winds. The pipe was passed to me.

I was glad he had used our good tobacco. It was rich and well cured. I repeated the symbolic ritual and passed the pipe to Chance.

As Chance took the pipe, he followed the same ritual. However, at each step he spoke in Wichita.

"To the Earth Mother who gave us life, who opened the great caverns beneath the earth to cover the face of the land with buffalo to feed her people."

"To the Sky Father who guards us, who makes the sun to warm the land and the moon to light the night."

"To the four sacred winds which bring the rain and snow that make the grass to grow to feed the buffalo and beasts of the earth and brings forth corn and squash to feed the people."

Finds the Buffalo sat in quiet reflection. "How is it you speak the words of gratitude to the Spirits? Are you Wichita? Your blue eyes say that you are not."

"I am a man of many peoples. I am not a Wichita, but I respect your beliefs. You are pressed hard by the white men and the Comanche. Your way is not easy. I speak to your Spirits that your way may not be so hard."

"You shall be called Many Peoples. I give you the welcome of my camp and the rights to seek horses on our lands. I will accept your gifts. You may gather as many horses as you want until the next full moon. At that time, you, Many Peoples, will bring to me one of every eight horses you capture. You will not keep any mares with nursing foals, and you will release the old ones to remain in peace. I will send Many Coups to help you and to make sure you keep our agreement. I ask for your word, Many Peoples."

I nodded my approval at Chance.

"I, Many Peoples, give you my word."

Finds the Buffalo opened the flap to his lodge, holding it open for us to walk out before him. He followed us outside. "Many Coups, you will go with them to help them find and capture horses until the full moon. Many Peoples will come with you to bring me one of every eight horses caught. No Wichita is to interfere with them or steal from them. You will be there to make sure they keep their agreement."

Many Coups entered his lodge to make preparations. His wife, Singing Bird, the daughter of Finds the Buffalo, would go with him. They loaded the things they needed on a travois and followed us to our camp.

On that day, I had seen a side of Chance I had never seen in all the years I knew him. I would never forget it.

———

Many Coups showed us a box canyon they used to trap horses. The canyon walls were steep clay and rock layered in broad bands of rusty red and pale yellow. Horses would not be able to climb out here. The canyon mouth opened to the west. A crude fence of brush angled in toward the center of the canyon from both sides. In the center was a pole gate of cottonwood trunks. It had obviously taken some time to build and showed signs of recent use.

The enclosed upper end of the canyon had a small spring that trickled down from the layered rocks into a small pool of clear water on the north side of the canyon walls. The brush fence and steep banks formed an enclosed area of eight to ten acres. This would be perfect.

Many Coups and Chance rode out together in the late afternoon. They found a band of about one hundred and twenty adult horses a few miles to the west. They were grazing undisturbed in a well watered valley covered with a thick blanket of winter cured grass.

The next morning, all of us rode out to try to drive the horses into the box canyon. Even Singing Bird rode with us. The curly tan buffalo grass was mixed with thick stands of blue grama grass which had cured to a light whitish tan, interspersed with much taller side oats grama. The seed heads on the side oats reached our stirrups. It was easy to distinguish because all the seed pods were on the same side of the stem and its winter colors of light pink and pale red. This was ideal country for horses and buffalo. One day it would be populated by cattle, but for now it was wild and free.

The frost sparkled on the dry grass. The air was sharp and crisp. Fortunately, there was no wind that morning, or it would have been much colder. Turkeys gobbled in the cottonwoods along a small creek and sand hill cranes flew high above us in the clear blue sky. A few deer skipped away into deeper cover as we rode past them. This was the kind of morning that made a man glad to be alive. My lungs drank in the pure wild air and my heart swelled within my chest. I remembered why I had fallen under the spell of Texas.

Many Coups led us in a wide circle around the grazing horse herd so that we would approach them from the west. He positioned us in a wide semi-circle, posting himself on the most southern end of the curving line. He had placed Chance at the northern end, with the rest of us spaced about evenly between them.

Many Coups gave the signal and our curving line moved slowly forward. A few of the wild horses looked up in alarm and began trotting away from us toward the east. The rest of the band followed the leaders. We were not to push them any faster than necessary. An older sorrel mare pushed her way, biting and kicking, to the front.

The herd formed into a rough oval shape with the lead mare up front and the older horses and foals toward the back. There appeared to be five or six dominant stallions that were scattered protectively along both sides.

The herd began to veer to the south. Many Coups beat his left hand against his deer skin leggings and clucked to the wild horses. Singing Bird, who rode next to him in line, did the same thing. The boss mare turned away, resuming an easterly direction. She tried to turn the band to the north, but Chance and the men on his end of the line imitated Many Coups behavior and managed to turn them back to the east again. Soon they were settled into a long trot heading straight into the wide mouth of the canyon. Once the herd had entered the canyon mouth, our line of riders collapsed into a straight line behind them. We were careful not to crowd them. The brush fence loomed gray on the horizon as it rapidly drew closer.

As the canyon narrowed, we tightened up our line to prevent them from turning back. The sorrel mare swung left, then right, but finally spotted the opening in the fence and set off for the gate at a lope. She bucked, passed gas, and gave a loud nicker as she ran through the gate, with the other horses following close behind her. They thundered through the opening into the other side. Many Coups and Chance jumped off their horses and ran to replace the cottonwood poles, closing the gate.

The horses circled inside the box canyon. Making a full circle, they found the gate they had entered closed behind them. The lead mare snorted at the gate and slowed to a trot and then a walk. They continued to slowly circle the canyon floor until they were convinced there was no was out. After an hour and a half, they settled and watered at the small spring. It didn't take them long to start grazing the thick tall grass.

I was amazed. "Many Coups, how did you do this so easily?"

"The sorrel mare that is the leader has been caught many times. We always let her go."

Over the next few days we rode through the horses. There were half a dozen that were too old to be of much use. They would be sorted off and released. There were eight mares with late born foals at their sides that we would also turn out. We decided which of the stallions was the best and decided to release him along with the older horses and mares with foals.

The next morning we managed to sort off the animals we were going to turn loose and get them out of the gate without losing the rest of the herd. Of course, the sorrel mare was released first of all. I had a feeling this would not be her last trip to this box canyon.

We began the process of preparing the horses for the long trail home. Chance approached Many Coups. "There are one hundred and four horses here. Pick the first thirteen horses for Finds the Buffalo."

Many Coups picked the five remaining stallions and eight good mares. He was pleased he had been given first pick. I don't think he knew that we didn't want the stallions. We would breed the mares to our Thoroughbred and cross bred stallions. We would have castrated the stallions that had been captured.

Many Coups used braided rawhide riatas like the rest of us. He rode his war horse alongside the animal to be caught and simply dropped the loop over its head and dropped the rope. Once he had all thirteen roped, he dismounted and approached each of them on foot. When he was close enough, he would grab the long end of the rope.

Feeling the pressure of the rope on their necks, the horses would pull away. Many Coups would jerk the rope, tightening it around their neck until it was choking the horse. They would snort and blow, pulling Many Coups across the ground. However, he would hold the rope with all his might.

A few he had to choke down to the ground. He would run up and slip a stout halter and lead rope over the horse's head. As soon as it was snugly in place, he removed the choking rawhide rope from the horse's neck. The relieved horse stood up and took several deep breaths before trotting away dragging the lead rope.

Some of the horses he didn't have to choke down. He kept pressure on the rope until they finally came to a standstill. He would gradually work his way up the rope, speaking softly to the trembling horse. Once he was near the head, he would allow the horse to smell the halter and gently stroke its neck with it. Once they had quieted, he would slip the halter over their head and release the rope around their neck. This process took longer, but seemed easier on the horses.

Cody and Nick roped our remaining horses, ninety-one in all. As the loop snugged down over the horse's neck, they would dally to the saddle horn and pull it tight. Once they quit fighting so hard, the other men and boys worked their way up the rope and gently talked to the horses. They would continue to talk until the horse allowed them to touch it. They would continue to pat and rub the horse, and allow it to smell their hands. Finally, they would slip a halter and long lead rope on to the horse. Once this was done, they would continue to talk to the horse, patted it a bit more and removed the rope from them.

When this failed, the wild horse would be roped by a second man by the back feet and tripped. Both the head and foot roper would move their horses gently to keep the wild horse down. This gave the men on the ground a moment to run in and put on a halter and lead rope. This way was fast, but rough on the captured horse.

Logan was running in to halter a tripped horse when he stumbled and fell face first into a fresh pile of horse manure. Gray was laughing so hard he ran right under the rope which caught him in the throat. The jolt sent him flying backwards a few feet. He landed with his rear squarely into another fresh pile of manure. We referred to them as 'the green brothers' the rest of the trip.

After two long, hard days all the horses were dragging lead ropes. Each time they stepped on the rope it jerked their head down and pulled against the nose band of their halters. By the end of a week most of them had learned it hurt their nose and head to pull against a rope. They were on their way to learning how to be useful.

There were a dozen especially nice yearlings that gentled down very quickly. These could be led behind another horse in just a few days. Several in the group claimed one of these young horses and worked with it every day.

Many Coups was ready to drive his share of the horses back to the village. Singing Bird struck their small lodge and loaded their belongings on the travois. Chance and I rode along with them back to the Wichita camp. Finds the Buffalo was very pleased with the horses. He gave the best stallion to Many Coups and a pretty mare to Singing Bird. We smoked with him, then rode back to the canyon. We were eager to be headed home.

The seventy-nine loose herded horses ran out of the open gate only to have their heads jerked down by the trailing ropes. They finally settled down into some semblance of order. The especially gentle horses were led behind their chosen owners' saddle horses. The loose herded horses followed the wagon, while the men kept them in place from both flanks and from the drag. The horses quickly learned what was expected of them and gave us a minimum of trouble.

We pushed the captured horses just enough to keep them a little tired each day, just enough they wouldn't think about running away. They continued to learn about the lead ropes and learned to turn their head slightly to avoid stepping on the rope.

We made just short of twenty miles the first day. We camped where we found good grass and water. Two men were on guard duty at all times. Chance suggested that I had stood more than my share of guard duty over the years, and that he hadn't allowed a spot for me in the rotation. I started to protest, but just shrugged my shoulders and smiled.

In a week we made it back to Fort Parker. Brian, Kevin and Parker Adamson each got to keep the yearling he had been training as his part of the venture. We kept the horses inside the fort that night and slept in real beds and ate home cooked food. It was a nice change.

The next morning the wind blew straight out of the North Pole. Pellets of sleet peppered the ground. We thanked our hosts, told the Adamson boys goodbye and put the wagon down the river road at a good trot toward home. The mules had been tired from the pace of the trip, but sensed we were getting close to home and pulled with a will. The wagon tarp blocked much of the wind and sleet from me and I wrapped the buffalo robe around me.

The younger men had pulled out their heaviest clothes and coats. Some rode with wool blankets wrapped over them for extra warmth. It wasn't much fun for any one, so we kept the pace going. Finally, we reached the northernmost of my rail fenced pastures. There was plenty of winter cured grass and enough trees to provide wind breaks for the horses. We turned the loose horses in the pasture and left only the haltered and led horses for the others to take home. We were anxious to get out of the weather and to see our families, so we agreed to meet back in a few days to divide the horses when the weather was better.

The weather turned off cold but sunny with almost no wind. We met at the pasture and began dividing up the horses. The youngest men, including 'the green brothers', elected to keep the horse they were training plus one other. Chavez and Lucio were thrilled with the deal. Cody, Nick, Tanner Lane and Chance each got fifteen head. It was only fair as they had done the real work and the youngsters were mainly along for the adventure. As the horses didn't divide evenly, I got seventeen because I had provided the supplies. Every one seemed satisfied with the fairness of the trade. The extra cash or trade value of the horses helped us get through a financial rough spot better than most, plus we had enjoyed our shared adventure. And I had a new respect for Chance.

7

July 12, 1839, Angelina Creek, Cherokee County, Republic of Texas

MIRABEAU B. LAMAR, candidate for the War Party, had been elected President of the Republic of Texas. He had taken office in December 1838. Sam Houston, the leader of the Peace Party, was not eligible to be elected to consecutive terms. The Peace party had offered a political unknown who had garnered only five percent of the vote.

I didn't like Lamar. First, he hated my friend Sam Houston. Second, I loathed his politics. He was staunchly anti-Mexican and anti-Indian. The land titles Sam Houston had promised the settled tribes were invalidated. Lamar made it clear there was no room in Texas for either Indians or Mexicans.

In May, 1839, a Mexican agent named Manuel Flores was captured. He had on his person letters from the Mexican government to the various settled Indian chiefs who had been involved in Cordova's insurrection. The letters seemed to confirm that some type of alliance had been reached between Mexico and the Indians.

Lamar was infuriated, as was his crusty, Indian-hating Vice-President David G. Burnett. Lamar had called out the militia again with the intention of driving the last of the Indians from east and northeast Texas. The Louisiana Landing militia, as well as ours from Navasota Crossing, had been given orders to meet at the junction of Angelina Creek with the Neches River north of Nacogdoches. No fewer than five generals of the Republic of Texas led the expedition, including K .H. Dougal, Edward Burleson, Albert Sydney Johnston, and Vice-President Burnett. Only Burleson was a friend of Houston. Being a lowly lieutenant colonel, I felt like a penny in a pocket full of pesos.

We rode out fully equipped and armed, riding under the Lone Star flag. It had a huge lone white star, sitting in a field of blue, with a broad horizontal field of white above one of red. We carried it with pride, for we knew the price in blood that had been paid for it. But we carried it with dread for the job before us.

We reached the camp on the Neches July 12, 1839. Major Chance and I were part of a delegation sent to convey Lamar's demands to the Indians: leave Texas or die. He offered them safe passage with a military escort to Indian Territory.

The chiefs were startled and angry, as Lamar had undoubtedly expected. He had demanded an immediate answer, but they refused to leave.

The various Indian tribes consisted of Cherokee, Delaware, Shawnee, Kickapoo and what was left of the defeated Caddo. They had occupied a flat topped hill that was the site of a Cherokee village. The woman and children were immediately sent north.

On the morning of July 15, 1839, a Texan force of regular soldiers, militia and Rangers set out for the Indian position. The Indians repelled repeated frontal attacks. But while they were occupied in the front, a large detachment of Rangers had moved to the Indian's left flank.

The Rangers suddenly appeared over the top of the high ground behind the Indian line. The Indians raced across the flat topped hill and waged a stout fighting retreat down the heavily forested steep north slope.

The Rangers took cover at the top of the hill, but were held down by heavy rifle fire from the Indians. The Indians regrouped in a ravine a half mile to the north. The ravine provided an excellent defensive position. The ground sloped down toward the ravine, and rose in a long gentle slope behind it. The front slope was sparsely wooded and provided little cover for the Texans. The back slope was old growth timber that would provide good cover for a retreat.

The Indians were led by Duwali, High Chief of the Cherokee. He was the son of an Irishman and a Cherokee mother. An old man of eighty-three years with long flowing hair that had faded from red to gray, he had piercing blue eyes, weathered pale skin and freckles. Dressed in a dark blue military jacket and a red officer's hat given to him by Houston, the old chief was armed with a pair of pistols, a fine rifle and a sword also given to him by Houston.

While frontal assaults kept the Indians occupied, my regiment was ordered to hit the Indians in their right flank. I gave my orders quickly.

"Major Chance, take half the company to the left about two hundred yards and cross the ravine. Once across, you are to form a skirmish line."

"Nicholas. Excuse me. Captain Teel, take the rest of the company and assume a skirmish line on this side of the ravine."

"I will keep Cody, Chavez, Lucio, Gray, Tanner and Logan with me. Once the two skirmish lines are set, the seven of us will push directly up the bottom of the ravine toward the enemy. Our attack will be the signal for a general assault all along the front. Any questions? Then get moving."

Chance's company of about forty men disappeared out of sight to our left. Nick's company of another forty followed them. Once they left we followed using the troops along the front and the heavy cloud of gun smoke to screen our movement.

I saw Chance's company across the ravine kneeling six feet apart in three ranks facing the Indians. Nick's company was similarly arranged on this side of the ravine. My small party carefully climbed down to the bottom of the ravine.

We moved slowly toward the Indian position. The flanking companies moved forward even with us. We continued forward until we could tell from the sound of the gunfire that we were very close. A momentary shift in the breeze blew the thick gun smoke away revealing the Indians less than fifty yards before us.

"Skirmish fire by ranks. Fire!"

The kneeling men of both companies fired left to right into the ravine, followed by the second rank, then the third. By then the first rank had reloaded and fired again, followed shortly by the other two ranks. It was a tactic we had practiced many times.

Our assault on the Indian flank initiated a full frontal assault from the main Texan force. Our small group in the ravine took defensive positions behind rocks, logs and trees to deter escape in our direction.

The Indians broke from the ravine and began a fighting retreat up the long slope using the trees for cover. Nick's company crossed the ravine as did my small escort. We formed up with Chance's company and waited until the main body of Texans had crossed.

My regiment now formed the extreme left flank of the Texan force. We formed company front skirmish order three ranks deep. The lines walked six feet apart, almost shoulder to shoulder.

"At the walk, forward!"

We slowly, carefully swept through the forest. Although there had been some firing further down the line to our right, our companies only disturbed a stray hog and an armadillo.

Once we topped the hill, we could see rolling pasture land opening into a corn field of twenty acres or more. Duwali was now mounted on a fine sorrel horse with four white socks. He was arranging his men into a defensive position in the edge of the corn field.

Orders came down the line to advance on the double. We were about two hundred yards from the edge of the field when the Indians abandoned their position.

Duwali tried in vain to rally his men to turn and fight, but his horse was killed by multiple bullets and fell dead beneath him. He struggled to the edge of the forest behind the corn field. A bullet took him in the back just as he reached the trees. He raised himself into a sitting position leaning against a large oak tree. The rest of the Indians disappeared into the forest.

An army sergeant ordered Duwali to surrender. He wearily raised a pistol at the soldier in a last act of defiance. The sergeant sent a pistol ball through the old chief's head.

Later, as the troops reformed on the pasture, a member of some militia unit scalped the lifeless body of the brave old chief. The Cherokee believed that those whose bodies had been mutilated were condemned to wander the earth. They would not bury a warrior who had been scalped. The Texan commanders refused our request to retrieve his scalp and bury him with some decency. His body was left for the coyotes, crows and buzzards. More than one hundred Indians were killed. The Texans had lost three killed and seventeen wounded.

The last of the scattered pockets of Indians abandoned their homes and farms. They streamed across the Red River into Indian Territory and southeastern Arkansas.

The "Cherokee War" ended any meaningful Indian presence in a vast area of northeast Texas. The Texas Land Office rapidly accepted claims of the new settlers who poured onto the abandoned farms and homes. Many of them found fields they had not plowed, and crops they had not planted, with cabins and barns standing vacant.

8

March 19, 1840, Austin, Travis County, Republic of Texas

IN LATE 1839, PRESIDENT Lamar moved the capital from Houston to the little community of Waterloo on the Colorado River. It was renamed Austin in honor of the late Father of Texas. Lamar ignored warnings from Sam Houston and others that the location was vulnerable to attacks by Indians and Mexican troops.

The end of the threat from Indians in east Texas secured our eastern boundary. France recognized the Republic of Texas, as had the break-away Mexican state of Yucatan. This was soon followed by recognition by Great Britain and Holland.

Texas still faced threats from the Comanche in the west and northwest. Mexico continued to breathe threats of war along the southwestern frontier.

Texas Commissioners of Indian Affairs, William C. Cooke and Huge McLeod, sent emissaries to the Penateka band of Comanche led by Chief Muk-wah-ruh. All leaders of the Penateka were invited to meet for peace talks in San Antonio. The Comanche were told to exchange all of their hostages in return for gifts as a condition of the proposed peace treaty.

On March 19, 1840, sixty-two Comanche leaders assembled at a huge tent in the city square. The Indian Commissioners met with them, accompanied by a small bodyguard of soldiers.

The Penateka brought a handful of Mexican children and one white woman captive. The Commissioners challenged them that there must be other white captives they had not brought. At that time, Matilda Lockhart, the sixteen year old lone white captive, began to tell by-standers her story. She told of years of physical and sexual abuse. She removed the scarf that partially covered her face to show where her nose had been burned off. It left a grotesque blackened hole in her face. A woman listener screamed in horror, drawing a larger crowd. As more and more people crowded around and saw the cruelty of the Comanche, the crowd became unruly.

A member of the guard detail was rushed to summon the garrison troops to maintain order. The Comanche saw dozens of armed soldiers rushing toward the Council House tent. Fearing they had been betrayed, a young brave sprinted through the tent flap to find the way blocked by soldiers with bayonets. The Indians plunged a knife deep in a corporal's chest. Another soldier shot the brave to death. A general melee erupted. Weapons appeared from under robes. Knives, tomahawks, and pistols flashed. Rifles, bayonets and swords struck back. When the smoke cleared and the screaming stopped, thirty-five Comanche lay dead, as did seven Texans. The surviving Penateka were taken captive.

One Indian woman was released to return to her people to tell them to release all of their white captives or feel the wrath of Texas. The Comanche responded by torturing to death all the white hostages they held.

———————

The story of the "Council House Fight" spread like prairie fire among the various bands of Comanche and their Kiowa allies. By late spring, a great meeting of the People assembled in the Valley of the Hard Wood, or as the Spanish called it, El Valle de Palo Duro.

After much talk, it was decided to send a massive raid deep into the heart of Texas, a raid that would strike terror into the very soul of the Texans.

In late July, war bands large and small again gathered in the Palo Duro Canyon. Some bands even brought their women with them. They did not bring their lodges, for this was a war party, a war party greater than any in the memory of the People. The war band leaders chose Buffalo Hump to be war chief for this greatest of all raids. After two days of debate, the plan of attack and route were hammered out. The clear night air echoed with drums and war chants off the four hundred foot multicolored walls of the canyon.

In the purple predawn eight hundred Comanche and Kiowa struck the war trail. They followed the Prairie Dog Fork of the Red River to the confluence of the other tributaries with the main channel of swirling silt laden waters of the Red River. Where the great bend in the river turned to run west to east, Buffalo Hump led them south.

They crossed the gyp water Pease River. They skirted the territory of the Wichita, who hid from the enormous power of their enemy. The Comanche continued south to the head waters of Pecan Bayou which would lead them deep into Texas. They followed the banks of Pecan Bayou as it ran roughly east southeast. They took their time to let their horses graze on the strong green grass. When the clear waters of Pecan Bayou flowed into the larger Colorado River, the Comanche now were only a day's ride west of the Texan city of Austin. They made themselves invisible. The time had not yet come to declare their presence. Buffalo Hump led them across the Colorado River southeast until they were in the lush valley of the Guadalupe River. The area was thinly populated, but still the army of eight hundred mounted warriors went undetected.

On the morning of August 6, 1840, the town of Victoria on the banks of the Guadalupe found the whole Comanche nation pouring through their streets. A few early risers had sensed something wrong and warned the sleeping community just in time. The citizens took refuge in the commercial buildings along the main street. Weapons and ammunition were quickly distributed. A few unlucky Anglos were caught trying to reach the relative safety of the large buildings and were cut down. The Comanche found horses in stalls, small corrals, and stables in the town. They looted the hastily vacated houses and set them on fire.

By the time the war party made a concerted push on the citizens barricaded in the businesses, they found themselves caught in a withering cross-fire from both sides of the street. Every window bristled with multiple rifles. The second story galleries were lined with well armed citizens. In the confined space between the rows of buildings, the Comanche were not able to use their horses to their advantage. One impatient and imprudent warrior rode his war pony through the large glass window of a saloon. Neither the warrior nor the horse survived the defensive fury of the town's people.

Buffalo Hump saw that they had captured many horses. They had killed twelve Anglos and taken their scalps. It was a good time to declare victory and move on to the next town.

The mighty war band had suffered only a few losses in Victoria. Their thirst for revenge because of the "Council House Fight" was not yet satisfied. On the morning of August 7, 1840, they appeared outside the seaport town of Linnville on Lavaca Bay. It was the second busiest port on the Texas coast.

The Comanche stared in wonder at the great body of water. They marveled at the waves rolling in on the dirty yellow sand. They found the water too salty to drink.

Buffalo Hump redirected their efforts to rooting out someone to kill and something to plunder. They found the plunder in the large well stocked warehouses of Linnville. They bulged with things of wonder.

As they gathered up all the stray livestock and plundered the town, the citizen slipped away in anything that would float out into the safety of Lavaca Bay. They paddled, rowed or sailed until they were out of rifle range and watched as their town was destroyed.

Two Texans were killed in the town. A third was so enraged by the plundering that he saw fit to leave the safety of his row boat and wade in neck deep water to the shore. Before he set his feet in dry sand, his body was pierced by a dozen arrows. His scalped body lay washing back and forth in the tide surf, a deterrent to any one else foolish enough to try.

Here the Comanche spilled their rage. All day long, through the night and until late the next afternoon they took anything they fancied and destroyed the rest.

The horses and mules they kept. The few milk cows they slaughtered and ate, cooking them over the wood of their own sheds. The cats, dogs, chickens and hogs were killed for sport and for spite. They loaded pack mules with bolts of imported cloth. They dressed themselves in fine frilled English shirts, tweed jackets and top hats. A crate of ladies parasols made a spectacle as the world's finest light cavalry rode carrying pink umbrellas.

Once the shops and warehouses were emptied, they burned everything that would burn. Through this endless day and a half orgy of destruction, the helpless citizens watched in thirsty frustration from the safety of the bay.

Late in the afternoon of August 8, the eight hundred warriors rode boldly out of the town to the northwest. Their horses were draped in fine damask. The warriors were gaudy in their unnatural clothing. The deadly column rode away, a comically brutal site.

But they did not ride alone. A small company of Rangers from Gonzales had picked up their trail at Victoria. They shadowed them from a safe distance, hidden and unseen. The sweet taste of victory would soon sour in the Comanche stomachs.

The passage of the Comanche down the valley of the Guadalupe River had not quite gone unnoticed. A settler looking for strayed livestock had watched in amazed terror as the massive war party had ridden past in the distance. He rode to Gonzales to alert the Rangers.

There he found Ranger Captain Benjamin McCulloch. McCulloch gathered his company of twenty-four men. They kept the Comanche in sight and sent riders to spread the alarm and raise the militia and Ranger companies.

McCulloch's company was joined by a group of one hundred volunteers under Captain John Tumlinson. As the Comanche drove their stolen horses and plunder-laden mules northwest from the smoking ruins of Linville, the reinforced Rangers trailed them from a safe distance.

The Comanche were aware of the Rangers. They finally grew weary of the "yapping dogs" at their heels and detached a heavy rear guard to deal with them.

The Indians concealed themselves at a crossing on the small Casa Blanca River. The Rangers had stumbled too close to their quarry. A fierce brief fight ensued with modest casualties on both sides.

The Rangers and militia withdrew and the Comanche rejoined the main body. McCulloch and the twenty-four Rangers determined to continue to shadow the Indians while waiting for reinforcements. Tumlinson felt this was too dangerous, and took a defensive position near the Casa Blanca River. The company from Gonzales would proceed alone.

Militia Captains Caldwell and Bird soon joined McCulloch with another one hundred and seventeen men from the Gonzales area. The reinforcement increased the size of the force six fold. It was a tremendous encouragement to McCulloch and his men. The united force trailed behind the Indians like a pack of wolves.

Buffalo Hump had so far enjoyed great success. They had taken several scalps, hundreds of horses and mules, and plunder that exceeded the imagination. He was not about to risk such a historic success to deal with a handful of Rangers. Such a small force posed no threat to the Comanche.

On August 11, 1840, at a beautiful draw leading down to Plum Creek, Edward Burleson arrived with another hundred or so militia, plus thirteen Tonkawa scouts under Chief Placido. Major General Felix Huston, of the Republic of Texas' regular army, arrived on the scene to assume command.

Huston planned to divide his force into three contingents. This violated the long held military belief that a commander should never divide his force in the face of a superior enemy. Huston wasn't so much on military history as he was on fighting Indians. He was a hard man to like, but he knew his business.

A regiment of roughly one hundred men under Huston would maintain contact with the Comanche rear guard. Burleson with a hundred men and the Tonkawa would swing wide to the east and travel parallel with the main body of Indians. If the Texas rear guard succeeded in provoking the Indian rear guard into action, Burleson's men were to immediately hit the Comanche hard in their right flank.

A smaller company was sent wide to the west under Captain Caldwell. If both the rear guard and right flank attacks were successfully launched, they would attack the left flank to create chaos among the enemy.

On August 12, Huston sent his trailing forces much closer to the Comanche rear guard. The main Indian column was strung out, pushing hard to the northwest. Their heavily laden mules and stolen horses slowed their progress. But the Comanche had no intention of losing a single horse or mule.

One Comanche in the rear guard became particularly angry with the encroaching Rangers. He convinced several others to wheel around and attack the Anglos. The Indians fired their rifles and muskets from horseback and charged at the Rangers.

The Rangers opened fire with their rifles. The leader of the Comanche rear guard was wearing a fine beaver top hat. One of the first shots knocked the hat off his head. A hail of bullets rained down among the charging Indians. They turned and galloped back to the main Indian column.

This was the sign for which Huston was waiting. He ordered the Texans to charge the Comanche. Seeing that Huston had succeeded in engaging the enemy, Burleson's hundred men and Tonkawa allies fell upon the Indian right flank a quarter mile farther ahead of the rear guard. The flank attack caught the Comanche by surprise.

The Tonkawa, who fought on foot, threw themselves with violent rage into their mounted enemies. They would grab the running horses by their war bridles and jerk their heads sharply around, dismounting their riders. The Tonkawa then dispatched the fallen riders with war clubs and knives before they could regain their feet.

The flanking Rangers had spread themselves into a long line to create as much chaos as possible over a wide area. The Comanche column began to panic in their attempt to disengage from their attackers and save their plunder.

The attack by Caldwell's smaller company from the left flank completed the panic, setting the Comanche into head long flight. A running battle ensued and continued for fifteen brutal miles.

The results were mixed. The Texans had successfully driven the Comanche away, admittedly in the direction the Indians had wanted to go. Eighty-seven Comanche were killed, while only one Texan lost his life and seven were injured.

The Comanche kept most of their plunder. They had ridden to the sea and sacked a town, taking away horses, mules and scalps. They escaped with relatively light losses, totaling less than ten percent of their number. They lived to fight another day.

We did not learn of the raid or the battle until well after it was over. The thought of a Comanche war party of that size gripped my heart like an icy hand.

(9)

Spring 1841, Navasota Crossing, Leon County, Republic of Texas

THE INDIAN TROUBLES in Texas dampened the enthusiasm of new settlers. Where a river of immigrants had rolled down the Camino Real each spring, this year it was barely a trickle; only the most desperate or determined settlers came to Texas.

Our economy at Navasota Crossing settled into a subsistence pattern. We only grew those crops we needed for feeding our families and livestock. No one broke out new land or spent money unnecessarily. Coins of copper, silver and gold rarely circulated. When they did exchange hands, they traded at a premium and were hoarded again by their new owners.

Our Texas government had seen fit to print half a million dollars worth of bank notes backed by nothing, unlike the earlier bearer bonds. The new notes traded at a deep discount to coin or United States currency. Where Republic of Texas notes had been worth sixty-five cents to the dollar, they dropped to twelve and a half cents to the dollar. To make things worse, cotton was still too cheap to grow profitably.

We got by well enough. We ate beef every night for supper, with an occasional meal of venison. There was bacon for breakfast every day, with fresh eggs. We had some type of corn at every meal: corn meal mush at breakfast, corn cakes at lunch, and corn bread at supper. On special occasions, Nancy served fried chicken from a young cockerel, or stewed an old hen that had quit laying. On holidays, we found ham on the table.

In the spring we eagerly anticipated the early vegetables. Spinach, mustard and turnip greens were like manna from heaven when cooked with a little pork fat.

The summer months put green beans, black-eyed peas, squash and roasting ears of young corn. Late summer and fall saw okra, potatoes, sweet potatoes, watermelons, cantaloupe and pumpkins on the table.

We ground corn meal for the winter. Extra corn, still on the cob, filled our corn cribs. Potatoes, sweet potatoes, pumpkins, cabbage and onions filled our cellars. Tow sacks of dried beans and peas were hung from the rafters. Smoked hams and bacon filled our smoke house. The salt spring south of the settlement provided enough salt for eating, curing meat, and for our animals. Sorghum molasses and a little wild honey provided our only sweetening. Sugar was too expensive for now. Our milk cows gave us fresh milk, butter milk and butter most of the year. During the months when the milk cows were dry, we did without.

We raised a few acres of wheat making enough flour for biscuits once a week. Our neighbors grew enough tobacco for their own uses and a little to barter. I didn't use it and didn't grow it.

The one thing we were willing to trade for was coffee. We just couldn't seem to do without it. The coffee we got had been grown in Mexico or Central America. It came in tow sacks of beans to the Texas coast, up river by steamer, and over land to our store. I traded cow hides, jerky, pecans or surplus corn to get it. It was one of the few things people were willing to spend coin to buy. We roasted the beans and ground them ourselves. Sometimes we added a little scorched grain to make the coffee go farther. It was the only luxury in which we indulged.

A wooden box came for Richard Moore. He opened it at the store. What it contained would have a profound influence on our lives. Inside the box were three revolving pistols. They had cylinders that turned each time the hammer was cocked. When the trigger was pulled, the hammer would drop on a percussion cap firing one of the five chambers in the revolving cylinder.

The magnificent guns were Patterson Colt revolvers in .36 caliber. They were capable of delivering five lethal shots to a range of a hundred feet. One man now could have the fighting capability of five men, or even ten if he carried two of the guns. By pulling out the cylinder pin, a new loaded cylinder could be inserted in seconds. These guns Richard had ordered all came with a second cylinder. The loaded cylinder could have the five percussion caps pressed gently into position after placing it in the gun, or it could be carried with the percussion caps already in place. The second option presented the problem of accidental discharge, but saved considerable time when reloading. It was up to the user to decide if the time saved was worth the risk.

Richard gave one to his son, Tanner, and one to the young man he had raised since age ten, Gray Jamison. They practiced until all three of them could consistently hit a pumpkin at fifty feet. Once they had become proficient, they allowed the rest of us to try them. The gun was simple to load and easy to fire. They were much more accurate than the large single shot pistols we had been using.

Chance, Cody, Nick and Logan and I all managed to find the fifteen dollars or pesos it cost to buy one. I was amazed that both Aaron Chavez and Angelo Lucio had the money to order one each.

"Boys, where in the world did you find the money to order a gun?"

"Me and Chavez, we broke those horses we got up in the Wichita country. We both sold one to buy a gun. We can always catch another horse. We figure we can kill more Comanche that way."

Aaron and Angelo just grinned, but I knew they were deadly serious. They would never forget what the Comanche had done to their families.

———————

Perhaps the absence of immigrants on the Camino Real had been justified. Our friends, the Wichita, had grown weary of the intrusion of the white men into their diminishing hunting grounds. They could not push back the mighty Comanche, but the white settlers posed an easier target.

Tanner Lane rode in on a relay of horses and reined up in front of our house at dusk. "Howdy, Colonel! Something smells good in your kitchen!"

"Tanner, you seem to have a way of showing up just in time to eat. What brings you over here?"

"I got dispatches for you all the way from Austin. We got some over at the Landing, too. Looks like we'll be riding into trouble again."

He climbed down and we tended his horses and headed to the kitchen to see Nancy. "Why Tanner, aren't you a sight for sore eyes!"

"Miss Nancy, you're as pretty as a picture. What's for supper?"

"You never change a bit. Fried beef steak, mashed potatoes, gravy and corn bread. Does that meet with your approval?"

"Yes, Ma'am!"

I opened and read the dispatches as Tanner washed up. We were to proceed immediately to Louisiana Landing to join other militia companies for a major offensive against the Wichita on the upper Brazos. We would be under the command of General Edward Tarrant."

"Nancy, looks like the militia is riding again."

"Not again! When will they ever leave you alone?"

"I could decline to go. It's a volunteer force. Chance is second in command. He could lead them as well as I could."

"You haven't ever failed to answer when duty calls. I just wish it didn't call so often. Just make sure you get home. This baby is going to need a daddy."

My jaw hit the floor. "I figured we were done. This is mighty fine news!"

"You talk like I'm a hundred years old. Folks might be surprised an old Methuselah like you has fathered a child."

"I'm only fifty-eight. Abraham had Isaac when he was near a hundred." I grabbed her around the waist and we danced around the kitchen.

———

Due to the severity of the recent local Indian problems, we only mustered half the militia. The other sixty would remain behind under the command of Richard Moore. We saddled up our horses and half a dozen pack mules with supplies.

We arrived at Louisiana Landing to find General Tarrant already there with a hundred men. Tanner Lane was to command half of the Landing's sixty militia company. The other thirty were to remain behind to protect the settlement under the command of Captain Rob.

We traveled northwest along the Brazos. My men were most familiar with the area so they were deployed as scouts. Nick and I stayed behind to command the rest of our company. Chance took Tanner Moore, Gray, Logan, Cody, Chavez, and Lucio with him to scout.

———

"I'm taking Chavez and Lucio with me to the west. Cody, you take Gray, Logan and Tanner and head northwest. Be careful and meet back here at dusk."

Chance remembered the way to the camp of Finds the

Buffalo. They rode at a ground eating long trot. Just after noon, they caught the faint scent of wood smoke on the breeze. Soon, a thin haze of smoke was visible on the horizon. Chance slowed the horses and began a wide circle to approach the camp from the northwest.

On a small rise, Chance reined to a stop and fired a single shot. He attached a white rag to the end of his rifle and raised it above his head.

Within minutes, six Wichita braves road into view. Their leader raised his rifle horizontally above his head and trotted to meet Chance, followed closely by the other five braves.

It was Many Coups. He immediately recognized Chance and rode to meet him. They exchanged greetings. Chance quickly warned Many Coups of the danger coming to them. He urged him to ask Finds the Buffalo to relocate his camp north of the Red River.

Many Coups indicated he would take the message to the chief, but doubted he would leave. Chance urged him to at least send the women and children into Indian Territory. Many Coups said it was a decision for a chief, not him.

"My brother, Many Coups, if we meet in battle, I must fight you."

"I would be dishonored if you did not, Many Peoples." They turned and rode away. They would meet again soon.

———————

As the scouting patrol met just before dusk, they could hear gunfire to the southeast. They loped their horses until the gunfire was close. They spread out in a small grove of post oak trees and sent Chavez to see what was happening.

Chavez came galloping back. "It looks like three hundred Wichita have got the main column penned down. They have got them closed in from three sides with a steep creek bank at their backs."

"Let's go. All of you load both rifles, your old saddle pistols and your Colts. We're going to give the Indians a little surprise."

They reached the edge of a small island of timber just south of the fighting. Tarrant's men were penned down just as Chavez had described about a quarter of a mile away. The Wichita were mostly still mounted and pressing in from the northwest and south. Most of them were armed with bows, but several had rifles.

"When I give the order, we're going to charge into that bunch on the south. When we get in range, we're going to stop and use our rifles, then charge in with our pistols. If Colonel Turner is there, he'll know to charge when we hit. I don't know much about General Tarrant."

They worked closer through the cover of the trees until they were within easy rifle range of the fight. "Rifles, two shots from cover. Then on my order, charge with your Colts. Save your saddle pistols if you get in a jam. Pick a target. Fire!"

Seven Wichita fell dead. In the noise and confusion of battle, the direction of the attack had gone unnoticed.

"Pick a target. Fire!"

Several more Wichita were killed or wounded. They reloaded both rifles and sheathed them.

"Revolvers ready. Wait to fire until we are close. Pick your shots. At the gallop. Charge!"

The seven riders charged straight into the now depleted ranks of the most southern group of Wichita. When they were within fifty feet, they began firing their revolvers.

When the Wichita turned to repel them, they were assaulted with the repeating pistols. General Tarrant saw the opportunity presented by this sudden distraction to order his whole force to charge.

The militia charged up the creek bank and the seven mounted men put the southern group into flight. The men from the creek wheeled into company formation in three ranks and began to pour a steady lethal fire into the exposed flank of the central group of Wichita. The seven mounted scouts swung around behind the central group, reloaded their revolvers and fell among the Wichita with a fury.

Finding themselves attacked from three sides, the Wichita

broke for the only avenue of escape to the north. Seeing the center section flee, the flanking Wichita on the north wheeled about and galloped away.

Tarrant had his men mount and pursue them. They didn't stop until it was too dark to ride further.

Returning to the battlefield in the dark, the militia tended their dead and wounded. Fifteen volunteers had died and thirty had been wounded. Nick Teel had taken a musket ball to the calf of his leg. It had entered from one side and exited the other. The exit wound was as big as a man's fist.

The Wichita had not been able to retrieve all of their dead when they retreated. Seven bodies were found, including the body of Many Coups.

Chance made sure they were buried in the Wichita fashion. He had them wrapped in blankets and placed face up with their heads pointed east. Any other position would have hindered their spirits from entering the next life. At the grave of Many Coups, Chance stuck the fallen warrior's lance point down at the head of the grave. This indicated he had died in battle. He placed his war bow and shield in the grave before it was filled. At least Chance had not been the one who had killed him.

The "Wichita War" effectively ended organized raids from the Wichita against the white settlers. Occasionally raiders would slip down to steal horses or burn cabins, but the days of the Wichita as a threat in Texas were ended.

───────────

In the summer of 1841, under the misguided direction of President Lamar, a force of three hundred and twenty regular army troopers and volunteers set out to employ the force of arms to demonstrate the claim of the Republic of Texas to far away Santa Fe. Santa Fe had never been considered by anyone to be a part of Texas, but Lamar and others thought Texas should lay claim to all Mexican territory north of the Rio Grande all the way to distant California.

The "Santa Fe Expedition," as it was called, was led by General Hugh McLeod. They became lost in the great vastness of the high plains. Finally, the starving expedition stumbled into Tucumcari in Mexican territory. There they were met by Mexican troops, arrested and taken to Santa Fe.

From Santa Fe, the demoralized Texan prisoners were marched down the Pecos River, across the Rio Grande, through the heart of Mexico to Mexico City. They then were marched east to the dreaded Perote prison near Vera Cruz.

———

Lamar's ambition had far exceeded his grasp. The citizens of Texas were tired of the constant warfare they had endured under Lamar's policies. Perhaps war with the Indians had been necessary and inevitable; perhaps it had not.

The Republic's constitution made it impossible for him to serve successive terms of office. Lamar's hand-picked War Party candidate was David G. Burnett. He was one of a handful of Texans I truly disliked. Our old friend, Sam Houston, ran for the Peace Party.

The campaign was rough, even by Texas' standards. Burnett accused Houston of being a drunken half-Indian coward. Houston responded by referring to Burnett as "that hog thieving little Davey." Burnett unwisely and repeatedly challenged Houston to a duel. But the experienced duelist had no heart to kill his loud mouthed accuser. He declined on the basis that he never "fought downhill." His refusal to duel further incensed Burnett who increased the acidity of his rhetoric.

Captain Rob seemed to sum up many Texans' sentiments well. He said it was "better to have Sam Houston drunk in a ditch than Lamar and Burnett." I personally supported that summary of the position. When the election came on December 13, 1841, Sam Houston beat Burnett by a three to one margin. All across Texas, people celebrated the great man's victory.

10

March, 1842, Navasota Crossing, Leon County,
Republic of Texas

I HAD TAKEN ADVANTAGE
of fair weather to get some early spring planting done.
Cotton prices had rallied to ten cents a pound. I would try
to plant twenty acres of cotton. My stepsons, Marcus and
Lucius, both intended to plant ten acres each, as did Cody
and Nick. Chance only kept his range land. He had found
the plow did not fit his hand. He ran cross bred cattle and
horses.

I had only turned under a few rows when Aaron
Chavez galloped up on horse back. "What is it, Aaron?"

"Your wife said the baby is coming now and for
you to hurry. You ride my horse, I'll stay and plow."

Jumping on the saddled horse, I put him into a full
gallop along the river road. I sent dirt flying as I turned
through the gate and bailed off the horse for Angelo to
tend. I could hear an infant crying from the house as I
bolted through the kitchen door. The doctor met me on
the stairs.

"Congratulations, Reverend. It's a fine healthy
boy."

"How's Nancy?"

"She's fine. Since this wasn't her first baby, he

didn't wait around to get here. Go on up. Everything is fine."

I bounded the stairs two at a time to our bedroom. "Nancy?"

"Look at our baby boy." She turned back the edge of the blanket to show me a red headed infant, pitching a very good fit. We named him David.

———————

Terrifying news arrived soon after David was born. On March 5, Mexican General Adrian Woll had crossed into Texas with fourteen hundred Mexican troops and captured Refugio and San Antonio. He had allowed his men to loot what they wanted, taken one hundred Texans as prisoners and retreated leisurely back to Mexico. Texas had been caught flat footed and could not even mount a military response.

In an outrage against Tejanos in general, the Anglo population of San Antonio forced the venerable Juan Seguin and his family to leave the city. The hero of the Texas Revolution was hounded out of Texas all the way to Mexico. It was a sad chapter in Texas history.

President Houston called a special session of the Republic's legislature, but set the date for June 2. He promptly relocated the capital from Austin to Washington-on-the-Brazos. Austin was only seventy-five miles from San Antonio. I wrote to Houston questioning the delay in the special session.

The Honorable Sam Houston
President, Republic of Texas

April 14, 1842

Dear President Houston,

I hope this letter finds you well, old friend. Nancy and I, along with all the men who served under you in the Revolution are so pleased that you are again our President.

Our family is well and prospering.

I will get right to my point. There is much disrespectful talk about your decision to schedule the special session so long after the intrusion of Mexico upon our sacred soil. I trust you implicitly and would appreciate knowing your thoughts. Please understand that you now, and will forever, enjoy my fullest support and pray that God's mighty hand will guide you as you lead our Republic.

Your servant and friend,
Lieutenant Colonel Aaron Turner
Navasota Crossing

In two weeks I was pleased to receive a reply.

Lieutenant Colonel Aaron Turner
Commanding Officer of Militia
Navasota District, Republic of Texas
Navasota Crossing, Leon County, Republic of Texas

April 28, 1842

My dear friend and brother in arms,

I appreciate your letter. Many of my old friends have made the assumption that I am a doddering old fool. I deliberately set the date for the special session to allow tempers and tensions to cool. Were the Republic's Congress now in session I can assure you there would be an immediate call for war. I hope by delaying the session that reason will prevail over passion.

Poor Texas. She is so vast in land and natural resources, but devoid of the means to exploit those riches or even to defend herself.

We are not militarily able to enter into a full scale

war with Mexico. Our enemies south of the border know it. They should like nothing better than to goad us into open hostilities.

I can not express to you how much I appreciate your unwavering support at a time when many would stab me in the back.
God bless Texas!

Your friend and servant,
Sam Houston
President, Republic of Texas

I was humbled by the great man's response. I understood his position and supported it fully. Houston could have given in to the public's cry for vengeance and made every one happy. But in his wisdom, he had rather do what was in the long term best interest of Texas and be thought a fool. It took a man of great principle to do what he had done. My appreciation of him was even greater than before this crisis. We began to drill the militia and prepared for the storm to come.

––––––

The special session was called to order June 2, 1842. Congress declared a state of war existed with Mexico. They instituted a mandatory draft of one third of the male population. They voted to sell $10,000,000 in land to fund the war, and appointed Sam Houston to lead the army.

President Houston waited until the last possible day to sign the legislation. But rather than sign it on July 22, he vetoed it. Congress had already disbanded and could not over-ride his veto. They had gone home to get ready for war.

Houston, as he had expected, was the object of public outcry ranging from polite doubt from his friends to hatred and charges of cowardice from his enemies. He had fallen on his own sword to save the Republic.

Only the President could call a special session and the legislature was not scheduled to reconvene any time soon. Houston had bought Texas valuable time to grow stronger before entering the war that he knew was inevitable.

The Mexican government was stunned. They had calculated that the war-like pride of the rebellious Texans would have thrown them into a war the Texans could not hope to win. They had underestimated the wisdom of the "Raven."

————

Houston wasted no time in reorganizing the Texas government. He reduced salaries, including his own. He cut budgets, and took drastic steps to put Texas on a financially stable footing. He rightly considered Austin, isolated on the western frontier on the banks of the Colorado River, to be too vulnerable to depredations by both Mexicans and Comanche. He relocated the capital to Houston.

The Mexicans were determined to provoke a fight. They would try again. On September 11, 1842, General Woll, leading a thousand infantry and five hundred cavalry, again captured San Antonio. He had caught the District Court in session and captured sixty-seven Texans including several attorneys and judges. Captain Rob offered to send them a few dozen more lawyers for good measure.

Learning of the Mexican invasion, Captain Matthew Caldwell left Gonzales with two hundred and twenty-five men. They were joined by a Ranger company under Captain Jack Hays of fifteen men.

The Texans surprised a large detachment of Mexican troops on the east bank of Salado Creek between San Antonio and Austin. In the sharp action that followed, sixty Mexicans were killed and one Texan died. The surviving Mexicans made a hasty retreat to the safety of San Antonio.

General Woll responded by sending eight hundred and fifty men with two cannon to pursue the Texans. Unknown to both the

Texan and Mexican forces another reinforcement of Texas militia arrived in the area.

Fifty-four volunteers commanded by Nicholas Dawson from Fayette County arrived to find themselves in the rear of the Mexican army. Woll detached four hundred men and both cannon to attack Dawson's force. Thirty-six of the Texans were killed, fifteen were captured, and three escaped. The victory at Salado Creek had been nullified by the Dawson Massacre.

Bowing to intense public pressure, Sam Houston authorized General Alexander Somervell to send a force to respond. November 25, 1842, seven hundred men marched for the border. They captured Laredo on the Rio Grande with virtually no resistance.

At that point, two hundred men returned to San Antonio to provide a screening force should the Mexican forces push back into Texas. Somervell and the remaining five hundred Texans crossed the Rio Grande and captured the Mexican town of Guerrero.

Somervell's orders had strict limitations. He ordered his men to return to San Antonio. While two hundred obeyed their commander, another three hundred disobeyed orders and continued raiding in northern Mexico. Commanding volunteers always carried the risk of refusal to obey orders. Somervell took his two hundred men and headed back above the Nueces River.

The three hundred and eight men elected Colonel William S. Fisher as their commander. They pushed on to the Mexican town of Mier and stumbled into a Mexican army of over three thousand men. Several Texans were killed, a few escaped, and two hundred and sixty-one Texans were captured. The Mier expedition was a failure and a monument to the folly of pride.

The Republic was shaken to the roots. The Mexicans could

invade our southwestern border at will, and Texas was unable to stop the depredation. The Lone Star flag was stained with defeat.

With Mexico at our throats from the southwest, and the Comanche threatening settlements from the west and northwest all the way to the coast, Texas suddenly seemed bare and vulnerable.

We gathered our crops with our rifles at our sides. We kept scouting patrols on the watch. We drilled the militia. And we prayed: "God save Texas."

11

March 25, 1843, North central Mexico

THE FATE OF THE MEN of the Mier Expedition was still unfolding. During the brutal march across the harsh lands of northern Mexico, the Texans had attempted to escape. They had been easily recaptured, but would pay a price for their attempt.

A clay pot was filled with two hundred and forty-four white beans and seventeen black beans. Each man drawing a black bean was taken outside and shot.

The story of the atrocity did not panic the Texas Republic, but caused a slowly building anger that, when it reached its peak, would not easily be quenched. The militias at Navasota Crossing, Louisiana Landing and the new unit at Fort Parker trained for the day we all knew was coming.

Diplomats from both Texas and Mexico negotiated a truce on June 14, 1843, to begin January 1844. The legislature passed a bill over Sam Houston's veto, claiming all Mexican territory north of the Rio Grande all the way to the Pacific Ocean.

Nancy and I laughed at the absurdity of the law. "We can't even hold together the piece of Texas we claim now, and they want to claim all of it to the Pacific!"

"Are we ever going to know peace here?"

"Nancy, I have always hoped so. I think we will know peace, some day. But I don't know if we will see it in our lifetimes."

———

In Washington, United States President John Tyler opened annexation talks with the Republic of Texas' ambassadors. If Texas was to become part of the United States, its great strength would help Texas find the peace that had proven so elusive.

In December 1843, an offer of annexation was sent to the Texas Congress. The proposal would allow the United States to claim all public lands and assume all debts of Texas. The annexation offer was pushed by United States Senator John C. Calhoun, a long-time enemy of Sam Houston. He wanted Texas to enter the United States as a "slave state" to strengthen the position of the southern states in Congress. Houston saw the danger of using Texas as a bargaining chip, and he felt the terms were not favorable to Texas. He urged Texas to decline. The proposal to accept the annexation passed the Texas legislature by a ninety percent margin and was returned to the United States Congress for ratification.

———

The summer of 1843 was not kind to crops in Texas, for it was a summer of scorching drought. Our corn got off to a decent start and made it to knee high before the rains stopped. The cotton never really had a chance. It was dead before it had four leaves.

The few scattered rains that did come kept the struggling corn barely alive, but there would be no cotton crop that year. The corn was stunted, about shoulder high. The shriveled stalks had only one partially filled ear.

When we finally harvested the corn, our yield was only a fourth of normal. We would not have enough to feed ourselves and our livestock through the winter. The potatoes, sweet potatoes, beans, and peas were hardly worth harvesting.

Nancy had kept Lucio and Chavez busy hand watering her garden with buckets and dippers, so we had tomatoes and squash and fresh beans. The hot dry days had caused the orchard to drop its fruit.

"I'm worried we don't have nearly enough to get through the winter."

"Me, too, Nancy. On top of everything else, there isn't enough forage for the livestock, either. The price of cotton is way up, so I'm going to sell the cotton we've been storing."

———

Chavez and Lucio cut down the timber we needed to build two rafts to float our cotton to market. I hitched up the spiked tooth harrow and ran it across the parched fields and broadcast about twenty acres of oats. It took a bushel to the acre to sow the oats, but one good rain could provide some grazing. I was gambling on a fall rain. We floated the cotton down to the confluence of the Navasota and Brazos rivers where we met Captain Rob and the *Brazos Belle* at Jared Groce's plantation. The mood there was somber, as Groce had failed to produce a single bale on the thousands of acres his slaves farmed. Rob was his cheerful self as we secured our rafts behind the steamer.

"Colonel, that's the only cotton I've seen all year. You been hidin' it?"

"It's a few years old, but still good. We've been storing it until the price got better. Looks like we'll need the money it will bring this year for feed and groceries."

"Folks at the Landing are pretty gloomy, too. Mr. Applewhite already sold off some of his slaves. Says he can't feed the white folks, much less the darkies."

When we reached the coast, I was able to sell all forty bales for about $75 in silver each, plus $40 for all the logs. I bought ten large barrels of corn meal for $22 a barrel, sixty sacks of shelled corn at $6 a bag, a dozen sacks of oats for $5 per fifty pound bag, some coffee, sugar and molasses.

At Louisiana Landing, I had to borrow two of Mr. Applewhite's wagons to haul our feed and supplies home. He sent two slaves with us to bring them back. There was now a new community forming at the mid-point between the Navasota and the Brazos. There was a cluster of cabins, a small inn, a store and a church. Our country was growing a little in spite of itself.

Captain Rob and I had talked with Mr. Applewhite and the Lane brothers about the shortage of food we all faced this winter. There weren't great numbers of wild cattle or horses to be claimed in our area any more.

"I guess we could slaughter more of our breeding stock to get us through the winter." Tanner offered.

"We've worked so hard to breed them up from those rangy longhorns; I hate to kill them for food." Mr. Applewhite complained.

"I've been thinking there are plenty of buffalo up between the upper Brazos and the Red River. The Wichita have been moved to Indian Territory. Maybe we could take a trip up that way to hunt buffalo."

"You boys count me out. I'll stay here and keep the slaves from runnin' off. But I'll put up the freight wagons, drivers and supplies for a share of the meat and hides."

We agreed to meet back at the Landing on December 27 for the hunt. It wasn't hard to sell the idea at home. Chance, Nick, Cody, Tanner Moore, Gray, Logan, Chavez and Lucio all wanted to go. Richard Moore and the remaining men would protect the settlement in our absence. We sent word to Fort Parker, and the three Adamson boys decided to join us. They would meet us at the Landing.

When we arrived on the Brazos, we found Rob, the three Lane brothers, and the Adamson boys waiting for us. There were four heavy freight wagons hitched to teams of four solid draft mules each. The wagons had barrels of salt to cure the meat and hides, and enough provision for the whole expedition. There was also a Negro driver for each wagon. Counting the slaves, there would be twenty of us who could handle a gun in case we ran into trouble.

The brisk January air was still and clear. Chance, Cody and Nick had found a herd of a couple of hundred buffalo sheltering in a broad valley. They had worked quietly up to the buffalo herd on hands and knees in the tall grass. They were within fifty yards of the great shaggy beasts.

They grazed quietly; their breath hung like wreathes of steam around their lowered heads. After watching their behavior for a while, it became apparent that this herd was led by an old cow buffalo. She showed that she was the dominant animal in the herd. The others would follow her lead. If she spooked and ran, the others would follow. She would have to be the first to die.

It was decided for Chance to take the first shot. He and the others spread out in the grass. Chance used a pair of crossed sticks to steady his rifle. He waited until he had a clear shot. She quartered slightly away from him. Aiming so that the .50 caliber slug would enter her unprotected abdomen and travel unhindered forward into her heart and lungs, he held his breath and squeezed the trigger. The old buffalo lurched forward and sprawled onto her brisket, blood foaming from her nose. Her legs kicked a few times and she lay still and silent.

The other buffalo sniffed at her and continued grazing. Cody picked out a young bull and dropped him cleanly. Nick followed with a nice shot on a fat barren cow. This continued until they had killed a total of forty-five buffalo, all bulls and barren cows, as we had agreed. This would be all the meat and hides we could handle.

When the hunters stood in the tall grass, the near-sighted buffalo snorted and trotted to the other end of the valley to continue grazing. When the wagons, mules and horses appeared, they disappeared over a rise, finally breaking into their peculiar rocking chair gait.

All twenty of us set to skinning and butchering the buffalo. All of the hides we stacked in a towering pile on one of the wagons. Zeke took half a dozen huge buffalo livers to the wagon for our supper. He drove the wagon back to camp, while the Adamson brothers had the job of unloading and staking out the hides near camp.

The rest of the men worked until dark butchering the carcasses. The tongues were salted and placed in barrels. The loin meat was set aside for fresh eating on the way home. The massive hindquarters and front shoulders were removed and piled on the waiting wagons. Other barrels were filled with buffalo humps and briskets and packed in salt to cure.

By dusk, the forty-five carcasses had been trimmed of everything we could use. We didn't bone out the ribs, but little else was wasted. Even before the last wagon left the killing field, the gray wolves and coyotes began to move in on the remains.

The fried buffalo liver and onions was a rare treat. It had been a long day and we were famished. Beans and strong coffee rounded out our feast on the prairie.

The barrels of salted meat were set out of the wagons to make room for setting the quarters up so that they would quickly chill in the cold night air. The loins were laid out on wagon sheets on the seats in short piles. They would keep well in the crisp weather.

The next morning, the Adamson boys returned to the hides. They had staked them hair side down. Each flesh side was given a generous dusting of wood ashes and salt to speed the drying and reduce the inevitable smell. They kept the scavengers chased away.

Logan, our carpenter, with Tanner and Gray to help him, built wooden drying racks for the meat from post oak tied with rawhide. They gathered an abundant supply of green branches and small logs which they stacked near the racks.

The rest of us cut the meat away from the bone and gristle into thin uniform strips and hung the filets on the drying racks. Once a rack was filled, a smoky fire was kept smoldering beneath it.

By noon, we were ready for our lunch. Zeke served fried buffalo tender loins in grease, corn bread and plenty of coffee.

"Colonel, remind me why we eat beef instead of buffalo," Tanner Lane grinned as he reached for his third steak.

"Hey, Cody? You like this better than horse meat?" Chance teased.

"Y'all just don't ever forget nothin' do ya'!"

After a short nap, we sharpened our knives and returned to our butchering. The drying racks were filling up, so Logan had to build several more. We were still not finished by dark.

"Well, boys, that's it. I can't hold a knife anymore. My hands are cramping."

"Hey, Zeke! What's for supper?" asked Tanner Lane.

"Sah, we got buffalo steaks fried jes' right, fried taters, beans and all the coffee you can drink."

We laid into the tender buffalo steaks and filled our bellies to bursting. The stars were bright in the clear cold air. Soon the whole camp was snoring in exhausted sleep except for those unfortunate enough to share two hour stands of guard duty.

By noon the next day, the last of the meat was off the bone and on the racks, slowly curing in the smoke and dry air. Each time the meat was turned, it received a light sprinkling of salt. The meat in the barrels was taken out and resalted, then repacked into the barrels. The two days in the salt had drawn much of the excess moisture out already.

———

The weather turned colder and clouds were seen banked up far to the north. We were on the edge of the Comancheria, but we hoped the Comanche were holed up in their winter camps along the edge of the cap rock a hundred and fifty miles away.

As I eyed the clouds, I called Rob to me. "What do you think, Cap? How long do you think we've got before that weather catches up to us?"

"Shoot, I don't know. I reckon early tomorrow, maybe?"

"That's what I'm thinking, too. It's time to get moving."

One wagon was piled high with hides and roped down. The salted barrels were arranged to make room for the drying jerky. We laid a clean wagon tarp on the bed of the wagon and carefully stacked the incompletely cured meat on it. Another clean tarp was laid over the mounded piles of meat. The disassembled drying frames were placed on top of the tarps. The wagon bows and canvas were replaced on the three wagons carrying meat.

We were on the trail a couple of hours after daylight. The mules were fresh and rested, as were the horses. We headed southeast following the Brazos. We made twenty miles that day, even with a late start. As we set up camp, Logan and the others reassembled the drying racks and restarted the fires. Every one not involved with supper or livestock, was busy placing meat on the racks.

We got up early the next morning and were headed out by daylight. The breakfast of buffalo steaks and real biscuits had been a great way to start the day. By midmorning, the wind shifted to the north, but the cloud bank was still some distance to the north.

We didn't stop for lunch, but ate leftovers passed around by Zeke. The wind picked up with a sharp edge to it. I turned my collar up and tied a bandana across my face. Soon pellets of sleet added to our misery. Encouraged by the cold wind, we made twenty-five miles before stopping.

A rugged bluff north of the Brazos shielded us from the wind. There was plenty of wood at hand, water from the river, and decent grazing in a meadow between the bluff and the river. We set the drying racks up again and struggled to get fires going under them. Soon the meat was drying again.

We cut some post oak trees to make a large three-sided tent with the wagon tarps. Nick built a big rock fire pit by the open side of the tent. He turned large flat stones on their edges behind the pit to reflect heat back into the tent. Zeke got another good supper started with the last of the buffalo steaks. The rest of us stacked logs near the pit to warm us through the night. It became obvious that it was going to be a very long, very cold night. We had to take special precautions.

"Cody, I want the horses and mules picketed with two stout ropes between those trees about thirty feet from the tent. Put hobbles on every one of them. Point their tails to the wind. Get a feed bag on all of them with some oats and corn.

"Nick, get some of the men and roll the wagons on either side of the tent and the livestock. Take the wagon sheets down. I'm afraid this wind will blow them to shreds.

"You Lane brothers drag twenty hides off the pile and give one to every man to put on the outside of his bedroll. The lice usually leave them as soon as the buffalo are dead and cold, and Lord knows it's cold.

"Chance, you make sure every man has his rifle and pistol with him. Make sure those slaves got theirs, too. Keep two men on watch by turns all night long, only an hour at a time. I think that's all anyone can stand. I doubt a raiding party would venture out in this kind of weather, but we can't take any risks."

All was set in order and we settled down to rest as well as we could. Lucio and Chavez took the first watch.

"Angelo! You hear something?"

"Si, by the meat racks. Lobos I think."

As they cautiously approached the racks, five large wolves were seen dragging meat off the racks. They were hungry enough to ignore the smoldering fire and the presence of men. They raised their rifles and both killed a wolf. The others scattered.

The racket woke the whole camp, except Tanner Lane who could sleep through anything. We checked the livestock on the picket lines and found them unhurt. We built the drying fires higher than necessary in order to keep future predators away, while Chavez and Lucio skinned their wolves.

The light sleet changed to heavy snow by morning; about six inches had fallen by breakfast. The bacon, corn cakes and coffee brought us back to life as we waited the storm out.

We made a rope corral around part of the meadow where the livestock could paw through the snow for some grazing under guard. The horse guards wrapped buffalo hides over their coats to block out the wind and snow.

The snow lessened as the day went by, but the wind continued to howl. The hillside and tent gave us decent shelter, and we weren't too cold as long as we stayed inside the buffalo hides.

The snow-covered ground would make traveling difficult and the wind would make it miserable. We had plenty of food. The jerky needed a little longer to dry, so we decided to wait another day.

The Adamson boys, Logan, Gray, Tanner, Chavez and Lucio found that the hides left on the wagon had frozen solid. With the snow covered steep hill behind the camp, they got an idea.

They turned the frozen hides flesh side down and used them as huge sleds to slide down the hill. Soon they had perfected their technique until they could slide halfway across the meadow at the foot of the hill.

Logan labored all the way to the top of the steep bluff. He launched himself into a downhill slide of breathtaking speed. His buffalo skin sled raced down the side of the bluff, across the meadow and continued across the thin ice on the Brazos. He broke through with a huge splash and a few cuss words.

We laughed until our sides hurt once we realized he wasn't hurt. As he shivered his way into dry clothes, I reminded him I had been trying to get him baptized for years, but I didn't think this would count.

_____

The next day, the sun was out and the wind was gently shifting to the south. We broke camp and headed home. The slushy roads slowed our progress to only twelve miles. We found a good camp site that was relatively dry with some grazing. The jerky had finished curing, so it was a relief not to have to fool with it again. We used the posts from the drying racks to make four good sized tents covered with buffalo hides.

The next day brought warmer temperatures and a drying,

steady south wind. The road was rockier making it easier for the horses and mules. We covered twenty-five miles that day, reaching Fort Parker by night fall.

After camping in the snow and slush, a bedroll in a cabin was mighty welcome. I discovered not all the lice had left the buffalo hides.

With the coming of day, we ate breakfast and divided out the Adamson boys' share of the meat. They only wanted one hide each and declined a share in the humps, tongues or briskets. I suggested they smoke the hides well before using them on their beds.

When we reached Navasota Crossing, we unloaded our share of the hides, jerky and salted meats. The Lanes and Rob expressed no interest in the salted meats, and declined on behalf of Mr. Applewhite as well. The wagons rolled on to Louisiana Landing.

Texas had come through for us once again. We should have plenty of food for the winter as long as we didn't get tired of eating jerky, salted buffalo hump, tongue and brisket.

12

February 1, 1844, Navasota Crossing, Leon County, Republic of Texas

THE SNOWS WHICH HAD fallen over the winter in the buffalo country had come as slow soaking rains in Leon County. Relatively mild weather had followed the rains, and the oats were poking through the ground. The green tips were a promise of grazing soon to follow.

We had kept the most valuable livestock near the fort, but the more common animals were herded under guard on a previously ungrazed large pasture a few miles north of the settlement. We built a small rough cabin there for Lucio and Chavez to live in while they tended the animals. They stayed horse back during the day and drove the animals into picket corrals at night. It was a big responsibility, but they were up to the job, and seemed to enjoy it.

We all celebrated when we learned that James K. Polk of Tennessee had been sworn in as President of the United States. He was a long time friend of Sam Houston and a staunch supporter of annexation of Texas.

John Calhoun kept making a racket favoring annexation because Texas would be a "slave state." Ninety percent of Texans were neither slaves nor slave owners. The only people I knew who owned slaves were Michael Applewhite and Jared Groce.

The concept of Texas as a slave state clouded the issue of annexation and involved Texas in the complex politics between the north and the south. The United States Senate rejected the proposed annexation of Texas on June 8, 1844. Texas was all dressed up with nowhere to go.

———————

We watched the livestock blossom on the rich oats pasture. Those that had roughed it out with Chavez and Lucio started to look better as the early spring rains brought up the native clovers, wild rye grass and weeds, and later, the strong native grasses.

We got our corn up to a good stand. Once the ground was warm enough, we planted twenty acres of cotton with seed I had bought. The rains fell generously, and the cotton and other crops prospered.

We picked forty bales just from our twenty acres. Nick and Cody had good yields, as did Lucius and Marcus. It would take three rafts to get it down river. While we were building the rafts we received tragic news from Tanner Lane.

Captain Rob had taken Stephanie and their sons, Charles and Sam, down to her father's plantation in November. They had taken a load of early picked cotton down to the coast. The coastal swamps near Brazosport had been especially thick with mosquitoes. The pests found their way into every crack and crevice in the *Brazos Belle* to make them all miserable. They were relieved to conclude their business there and head upriver.

On the trip north both Charles and Sam became ill. They had high fever with shaking chills. Neither boy would eat. Both began to vomit. They complained of horrible back pain.

Stephanie was obviously worried. "Rob, please stop at Papa's plantation as soon as we can. These boys have to see a doctor."

Rob had his crew build all the steam the paddle wheeler

would carry. He stayed at the helm, dodging sand bars and snags, leaving navigation to the first mate only long enough to go below and check on the boys. The steamer tied up at the wharf at Groce's plantation.

Rob had signaled his unexpected arrival with the steam whistle. He saw Mr. Groce himself riding his gaited horse to the wharf.

"Captain Rob, no one is to set a foot off your boat. What do you want?'

"Your grandsons are both really sick. We need a doctor!"

"Nobody is getting off that boat! Cast off and move out to the middle of the river."

"Are you crazy? We need help! Send for the doctor."

"I'll send for the doctor, but if you don't move that boat away from the wharf, I'll burn it to the waterline!"

"Your own daughter and grandsons need help. What's wrong with you?"

"It's not what's wrong with me, but what is wrong with those boys, God bless 'em. There is a yellow fever outbreak on the coast and sounds like they've got it. You get off here and me and my family and a hundred slaves could die. I'm sorry."

Stephanie had come to the bridge. "Papa!"

"I'm sorry, girl. That's how it has to be. We'll float out what things you need and try to get a doctor out there, but you aren't setting foot off that boat."

In disbelief, Rob turned to his crew. "Cast off and anchor fore and aft mid-stream."

———————

By afternoon, Stephanie had fallen ill. Rob knew all about yellow fever. He had it in Louisiana years ago. His father-in-law was right about it what it was. And everyone lived in dread of it, except those who had survived it, for you couldn't get it twice. It all fit together now. But what could he do?

100

"Stephanie, your daddy says it is yellow fever, and I expect he is right. If he is, we are in for a bad time. I had it a long time ago and can't get it again. I'll take care of you and the boys. It'll be alright."

"I can't understand Papa acting like that."

"He's scared of it like everybody else."

Stephanie's fever climbed higher and her back pain and chills wracked her body. Rob went below to have the crew adjust the mooring line. They were all gone, as was the steamer's row boat. Rob made the needed adjustments himself. He didn't feel it necessary to tell his wife about the crew's departure.

Late that day, both boys spiked a fever. Before the night was over they both experienced multiple seizures. By morning, both boys looked better, but Stephanie was much worse. He managed to get a little food and water down the boys. As the sun set, the fever of all three went up and up. Both boys had bleeding from their mouth and nose. The whites of their eyes turned dark yellow. They began to vomit up blood, the dreaded "black vomit" of yellow fever.

Stephanie's illness was only a day behind the boys. She rapidly developed the same symptoms. She was delirious, talking out of her head. Sam's breathing became shallow. His pulse was rapid and weak. He was gone by noon. Charles followed him in death a few hours later.

Rob was overwhelmed with grief. The little boys had been the sunlight of his days, and they were gone. He wrapped their lifeless bodies in blankets and carried them out on deck.

Stephanie lapsed into a coma that night and was dead before daylight. He wrapped her in a large shawl and laid her on the deck next to the boys.

He went to the engine room and fired up both boilers. He took an ax and chopped through the anchor cable allowing the steamer to drift down stream. By the time he reached the pilot house, there was enough pressure to turn the *Belle's* bow down river.

Once under way, he stoked the boilers to the maximum pressure they would withstand. He pushed the little steamer down the muddy Brazos with reckless abandon. He left the pilot house only long enough to refuel the boilers. As shadows lengthened, he approached the wharfs in the area of the coast called Brazosport that he knew so well. He blew the shrill steam whistle to warn other vessels out of his way.

He steamed past the brackish flats out into the deep water of the bay. Breaking open a small barrel of coal oil, he spread it over each deck of the tidy white steamer. He opened a furnace door and rolled a large ember onto the deck, igniting a puddle of coal oil. As the fire quickly spread from deck to deck, he sat weeping, holding the bodies of his wife and sons. The flames rose a hundred feet in the salty night air. The funeral pyre was visible to everyone for miles along the coast. The heat buckled the metal plating below the water line. The waters of the Gulf of Mexico rushed in, extinguishing the flames and sending Rob and his loved ones to their graves beneath the waves.

13

January 15, 1845, Natchitoches, Louisiana,
United States

CODY AND NICK TEEL
had received a letter that their mother was in failing
health in Natchitoches. They loaded their wives and
children into a large wagon drawn by six matched draft
mules. Chance and Amanda had decided to join them
so he could see his family, too. They had a heavy freight
wagon drawn by six big bay mules. The irrepressible
Kassie Teel drove one wagon, and Amanda drove the
other. Cody, Chance and Nick loose herded twenty-two
horses they planned to sell in Natchitoches.

With the extra mules, the wagons made good
time. With an early start and a long day, they pushed
all the way to the small community that had grown up
where the Camino Real crossed the Trinity River. There
was still a ferry, plus a new blacksmith shop, a store and a
few houses. They penned their stock in the corrals behind
the blacksmith shop and paid for hay and feed. They set
up camp at the edge of town.

"This place sure has changed hasn't it," Nick
reminisced.

"This was the first place I ever had to kill another

man, the night the Karankawa attacked," Chance added thoughtfully.

"And this place dang near got me killed, too." Cody said, grabbing the scar above his left ear.

They told the children the less scary version of the Karankawa attack and their exploratory trip into Texas. The idea of huge naked tattooed Indians with six foot bows was enough to keep them interested. But none of the three men slept well that night, as ghosts of days gone by haunted their memories.

———————

Louis bon Chance sat in a rocker on the front porch of his store. "Got your letter. Heard you was comin'. Let me meet your wife and my grandchildren."

Chance hugged his father around the shoulders and introduced Amanda and the children. "I've missed you, Papa." The children were shy at first, but quickly took a liking to the lively old man, as they did to their grandmother.

Cody and Nick found their mother waiting at her cabin on the north edge of Natchitoches. She already knew Kassie, but was introduced to their children and Cody's wife, Miranda, and their children.

"Nicholas, you got a fine bunch of kids. That boy, Jake, reminds me of your old daddy."

"Cody, you weren't but thirteen the first time you rode off to Texas. You've growed up, son, with a pretty wife and fine children. I'm proud of both you boys."

———————

Their livestock was all at the livery stable, including the horses they hoped to sell. Prospective buyers lined up to have a look at the saddle-broke mustangs and cross bred horses they had to offer.

Buford Pendergrass, a large red-faced cotton planter and

gambling man, pushed his way to the fence. "Who owns that tall sorrel with the blaze face?"

"I reckon that's me, Cody Teel. He ain't for sale."

"I don't want to buy him from you, sonny. I want to set up a race between him and my horse, Thunder."

"I didn't come here to race. Do you want to buy some horses or not?"

"Tell you what I'll do, sonny. Let's set up a race from the north edge of town to the south. It's about a mile and a quarter. The winner gets the other's horse. What could be fairer than that?"

"I told you, I don't want to race."

"Tysoe, lead Thunder up here." A skinny Negro youth led a magnificent coal black stallion to the corrals. It was obvious that he had excellent Thoroughbred breeding and had been well cared for and trained.

Cody's horse was also a stallion. He was the three-quarters Thoroughbred stud Colonel Turner had given him. Cody knew he was faster than any horse he had ever seen, so far.

Pendergrass' horse had never lost a race. He made a lot of money goading strangers into racing against him.

"Mister, I don't think my horse would lose, but if he did, I wouldn't want to give him up. I won't race for my horse."

"Well, I understand you being intimidated by a fine horse like Thunder against some Texas cross-bred. I'll tell you what I'll do. I'll bet you my slave here against my pick of six of the horses you got for sale. Is that scary for you, sonny?"

"You know, mister, you're mighty short on manners. I told you my name is Cody Teel. You call me 'sonny' again and you're gonna get a good ol' county tail kickin'."

"Ha! Now I got your dander up. Is it a race?"

"I just rode my horse in from Texas. You give him two days to rest up, and you got yourself a horse race!"

"Noon. Two days from now. My name is Pendergrass. I've been needing some new horses; don't sell 'em before the race."

Cody regretted that he had been baited into the race. He and Nick fed the sorrel good fresh oats and hay. They rubbed every sore muscle on his body, neck and legs, and walked him to keep him from getting stiff.

Natchitoches was buzzing with talk of the race. Louis bon Chance was the local betting agent. The odds were heavy against Cody's horse, being posted at five to two. Nick told around town that his brother was crazy for taking the bet. He predicted the sorrel horse would run out of steam before the race was over. The odds increased to four to one, much to Nick's delight.

The evening before the race, Nick packed the right front hoof of the sorrel with clay before walking him down the street, causing the horse to limp slightly. The odds went to six to one; then he cleaned the hoof.

The morning of the race, the sorrel was carefully groomed. Nick had one last incentive to give the horse an edge. One of the mares in their string had come into heat. It was early in the season, but these things happened sometimes. He led the mare with the sorrel stallion down the back alleys of Natchitoches and tied her to a tree twenty feet past the finish line.

Just before noon, both stallions were led to the starting line. The local sheriff looked them over and declared they were fit to run. Thunder wore an imported English riding saddle, with the slave, Tysoe, perched like a bird on his back.

Cody's saddle had been cleaned and oiled. His rifle scabbard, saddle pistols and any extra weight had been removed. Cody probably outweighed Tysoe by thirty pounds.

The long red clay street had been cleared of obstacles. People lined both sides of the street. The porch at Louis' store was packed. Miranda, Kassie, Mrs. Teel, and the children waited at the finish line.

Nick soaked a heavy strand of the mare's tail hair in her urine. He brought it with him to the starting line. Just before the race was to begin, he held it under the quivering sorrel stallion's nose. The big horse snorted and pawed the ground.

With the crack of a pistol, the race was on! Thunder held a slight lead of half a length most of the way. Near the mid-point, Cody used his spurs for the first time. The sorrel drew even with Thunder. With two hundred yards to go, Cody gave a Comanche war yell, and the sorrel dug in and pulled slightly ahead.

Tysoe applied the whip liberally to Thunder who responded like the champion he was. He regained a slight lead. Down the last hundred yard stretch, the mare gave a nicker. The sorrel dug in for all he was worth and surged forward to win by a full length.

The sheriff certified the results and people began lining up at Louis' store to settle their bets. Pendergrass stomped off to a local bar to drown his frustration, sending Tysoe with signed transfer papers.

Cody had bet $50 on the race, and received $300 in silver. Nick had bet $100, which had turned into $600.

They sold the horses for $50 each for the mustangs, and $75 for the crosses. They bought a fine strapping Spanish jack to take back home for raising mules with their best mares. They also picked up a surprise for Nancy from me.

When they were ready to leave, Tysoe showed up carrying a small bundle. "Massah Teel, I reckon you my new owner."

"I never owned a slave in my life and I don't want one now."

"Sah, I gots to go wif ya. You send me back, Ol' Massah say he gonna beat me fo' losin' the race. Sez it wuz my fault."

"You know anything about farming or driving a team?"

"Yassah, I sho do."

"Climb up there and drive for a while. I gotta think this over."

The trip back was a bit longer since the wagons were loaded with supplies, including a new cast iron cook stove and oven for Nancy. There was a burned out ruin where Man Who Laugh's Caddo village had stood. He and his people had welcomed us on our first trip to Texas. The cabin of our friends, the Campos, was vacant. Two more graves had been added at the edge of the woods and marked with their names. They had befriended us on that first trip. We made it a point to stay with them each time we passed. The land on either side of the Campos farm belonging to the two clerks and the alcalde was abandoned. They had been granted land on either side of the Campos to protect them. Now Mexicans were unwelcome by many people in Texas.

——————————

Shortly after their return, we received an important letter from the capital. I quickly read it and re-read it to make sure I had it right. I went to the gate of the stockade and began to ring the big brass bell. Its baritone voice rolled across the settlement, the forests and fields. Once a crowd had assembled, I went upstairs to speak from the second story gallery of our house.

"My friends, I have received word today from President of the Republic of Texas, Dr. Anson Jones in Houston. On February 28, the United States Congress passed a bill to annex Texas. On the next day, United States President John Tyler signed it into law."

A crescendo of yelling and clapping came from the settlers assembled in front of the house. Their reaction indicated that for them, this was a dream come true.

"Texas will be admitted as a state, not a territory. The United States will assume all of Texas debt, and Texas will retain all of its public land. If Texas chooses to do so, it may divide off four additional states. Finally, slavery will be allowed, but not above a certain line north of the Canadian River."

The cheering was thunderous. It was all we had hoped for and more. With the strength and stability of the United States, Texas should flourish.

I held my hands for quiet. "Gentlemen, please remove your hats as we give thanks. Oh, Lord of Lords and King of Kings, we raise our voices in thanksgiving today. We thank you for the prospect of peace and prosperity that annexation holds for the people of Texas. We exalt your name in praise. God bless the United States, and God bless Texas. Amen."

———————

It remained for the Republic of Texas to accept the proposed annexation. That done, Texas needed to draw up a state constitution, and elect state office holders.

By October 13, 1845, the process was nearing completion. The Republic's legislature overwhelmingly approved the annexation. Elections had been held. James Pinckney Henderson was to be governor. Sam Houston and Thomas Jefferson Rusk would be United States Senators.

The state constitution was adopted. It had some things about it that set it apart. Women would enjoy full property rights in Texas. The Republic's homestead protection would become state law. No banks would be allowed to organize in Texas. No ordained minister could serve in the state legislature. I didn't particularly like that last provision, but didn't want to serve anyway.

Mexico offered a peace treaty to the Republic of Texas if it would decline annexation. They feared the United States would be a grasping neighbor. Texas not so politely declined the offer.

Final approval of annexation by both parties came on December 29, 1845, with the transfer of power to occur February 2, 1846. An omen of things to come was seen when Mexico reinforced the garrison at Matamoras to six thousand men under General Arista. The United States responded by landing four thousand soldiers at Corpus Christi. Our peace would have to wait a little longer.

14

February 19, 1846, Austin, Texas, United States

ON A CRISP WINTER DAY, February 19, 1846, the Republic of Texas ceased to exist. The Republic's "Lone Star Flag" was lowered, fluttering into the arms of Sam Houston, who cradled it like a baby. The "Stars and Stripes" rose up the flag pole with military honors. Texas became the twenty-eighth state. The Lone Star flag was raised beside it as a state flag, the only state allowed to fly its flag at the same height as the American flag.

Texas in 1846 was an immense state. It began in the well-watered thick pine forests and red soils of the east. It opened to vast prairies along the coast and in the center, rich dark soil waiting to yield to the plow. Desert mountains rose in the southwest, and high unexplored waterless plains dominated the northwest.

The economy was essentially all agricultural. Cotton and corn grew anywhere a plow could open the soil, and sugar cane grew along the coast. Cattle were trailed east to New Orleans or processed into jerky, hides and tallow along the coast. Very few Texans owned slaves, and most of those who did had only a handful.

The common people had simple diets. Irish and sweet potatoes, black-eyed peas and dried beans, fresh vegetables, corn and corn bread, and beef and pork filled the plates of most of the people. They were mostly immigrants from the southern United States, with small pockets of Czechs, Germans, and Poles in the limestone hills and valleys west of Austin.

The population was overwhelmingly white, of English, Irish and Scottish descent. There were some slaves, fewer Mexicans, and a handful of free blacks.

Tyso Pendergrass fell into this category. Cody could not abide the idea of owning another man, so he had set Tyso free. He took up the name of Teel and lived in a small cabin on Cody's land where he worked for food, shelter and wages. He was one of the happiest men in the settlement.

Texans were largely Protestant, especially Methodist, Baptist, and Cumberland Presbyterian. All three groups were known to have "camp meetings" of a week or longer scheduled around farming activities.

I continued to minister at the Methodist Church at Navasota Crossing. We shared the building with the Baptists who met each Sunday after we were finished. This suited me well, as the Baptist minister tended to be a little long winded.

The school had out grown the church building. It had a tidy building of its own of white-washed sawn lumber and a wood stove. There were two teachers, one of whom was Nancy. The other was Mrs. Morgan, the carpenter's wife.

Texas even had two colleges. Baylor Baptist College was open in the new town of Waco on the Brazos. Nacogdoches was home to the Presbyterian affiliated Austin College.

One did not have to look hard to see the rough edges of Texas. The people here earned their bread with the sweat of their brow. It was not an easy place, nor a peaceful place. Mexican troops were massed along the border. And the Comanche still ruled unchallenged up on the plains.

Statehood celebrations were still in full swing when a new enemy appeared. Many people, especially the children, developed what seemed to be a bad cold. They had runny noses, congestion, sneezing, a mild persistent cough, and fever. It seemed to be contagious.

After two weeks of illness, it became apparent it was not just a cold, but whooping cough. It had been many years since it had circulated in Texas, so the younger population had never been exposed to it. What had been a mild cough became uncontrollable fits of coughing with a distinct whooping sound as the victim inhaled. Several cases had already appeared at Navasota Crossing. Nancy and I had it as children, as had our married children. Little David had just turned four. He began with the cold-like symptoms; we were not surprised when it became obvious he had whooping cough.

David's appetite was off, but he otherwise seemed fine until a spasm of coughing would hit. His coughing would begin slowly, becoming more frequent and violent until he would cough so hard he would vomit. Then the cough escalated with each breath until the whooping began. The episodes lasted several minutes and left David exhausted. We had him breathe steam from a kettle with camphor added to the water. It seemed to help some. The doctor gave him syrup made of whiskey, sugar, peppermint oil and a few drops of turpentine. It didn't seem to do much, but it gave Nancy something to do when the spells hit. David gradually got better, but if he exerted himself or got too hot, the cough would return for progressively weaker and shorter fits. Finally, after three months he seemed to be over it.

Immigrants were again crowding the Camino Real into Texas. The population was growing. Demand for our cotton, surplus crops and cattle was strong. United States silver dollars were once again circulating, with the ever present peso. Both contained one ounce of ninety percent silver, so they were fully interchangeable. Mexican two reale coins, worth two-eighths of a peso, were used as quarter dollars. It could get a little interesting with smaller change.

At annexation, Republic of Texas notes had been redeemed at market value of eight Republic dollars to one United States dollar. Land scrip increased in value as new settlers pushed into Texas. It was negotiable in value, set by the buyer and seller of the scrip. We generally held on to ours. We accepted it at favorable terms at the store and only sold any when a buyer was willing to pay a premium.

Our crops were good, including the cotton. Cody's farm hand, Tysoe, allowed him to double his cotton planting from ten to twenty acres. It was all the two men could manage, even with help at picking time.

We missed Rob and his family. Their death had been a tragedy. It hit home when we rafted our cotton down river to Jared Groce's plantation. Mr. Groce and his family had taken their deaths extremely hard, and felt if they had let them come ashore things might have been different.

We tied the rafts behind a little steamer called *Yellowstone* which had seen service ferrying troops during the war. Rob's ghost seemed to be with us as we climbed aboard and watched the paddles churning up the muddy water.

"Colonel, you remember that time the steamer blew up at Natchitoches? Me and Nick were just thinking about that and Captain Rob. I'll never forget our first trip to Texas with you and him and Chance. It seems a long time ago. Rob sure was good company."

"I remember how much he talked that night at that big feast with the Wichita. He had them laughin' and slappin' their legs. They couldn't speak a word of English and he couldn't speak Wichita."

"You two and Chance were building cabins at the Crossing when we brought the families out. The Trinity was flooded and we couldn't cross. It was a marvel to see that man build a ferry and get everybody across. He could do stuff nobody else could do."

"Lord, how he could talk. He could talk a squirrel into giving him an acorn just to be quiet." We all laughed remembering him. His death left a hole in our lives, but he walked many more miles with us in our memories.

15

April 4, 1846, Rio Grande River, United States-Mexican border

WHILE WE HAD BEEN dealing with whooping cough, raising corn and cotton, there had been increasing military activity along the border with Mexico. The Mexican army had been reinforcing the number of infantry and cavalry along the border. Zachary Taylor had responded by sending Major Jacob Brown to secure a strong foothold on the border across from Matamoros.

Brown built a strong six-sided fort with a double log wall filled with rubble packed between the walls. Heavy artillery bastions were engineered around the fort and firing pits built for the men around the wall. The powder magazine was dug into the floor of the fort like a deep cellar and the top was reinforced with logs and sand bags. They called their new construction Fort Texas.

Taylor sent cavalry patrols far up the Rio Grande to scout for enemy activity. One such patrol was a platoon of twenty dragoons under the command of a dashing young sergeant from Texas, Stan Branam.

He handled a horse like a Comanche and was a dead shot with the new Colt Walker six shot revolvers.

The new guns had nine inch barrels, measuring a whopping fifteen inches overall. He carried a matched pair in saddle holsters.

The potent new revolvers shot a .44 bullet from a reinforced cylinder that could handle a powder charge that would challenge many rifles. It was claimed that Sergeant Branam could consistently hit pumpkins at one hundred yards with either hand. The pistols were commonly called "Walker Colts" for Samuel Walker who had designed them for Samuel Colt. The rest of the platoon carried standard issue .50 caliber muzzle loading carbines and sabers, as did their sergeant.

———

A trusted corporal had been sent ahead of the platoon to scout. He came galloping back with a report. "Sarge, a whole bunch of shod horses crossed the river 'bout two miles upriver; the tracks still have water in 'em!"

"They're right on top of us! Ride back and find the lieutenant and the main column. Tell him we're going to try to shadow them without startin' a war."

"Column, right! Look sharp! Don't shoot unless I give the order."

The platoon wheeled by twos as it reached the place where the sergeant and the guidon bearer had turned. They had barely completed the maneuver when a large body of Mexican cavalry could be seen. It appeared to be about three hundred men, too many for Branam's small patrol.

"Sarge, we're in the stew now," quaked the frightened private carrying the guidon.

"Platoon, halt! We're in way over our heads. Form company front, five men wide, four men deep. The private and I will take the rear. We're gonna fall back on the rest of the company and get away from these Mexicans. They don't look none too friendly. If I give the order, you'll halt, and fight dismounted. Form up!"

Branam's commanding voice and handling of the situation calmed the skittish men. Once they were in formation, the order was given, "Forward at the trot."

A company of Mexican lancers peeled off the main column to follow the retreating American soldiers. They fanned out in company front, twenty men wide and four rows deep.

"Platoon, long trot."

The pace quickened and the Mexican's matched their speed. The razor sharp steel points of their lances gleamed in the sunlight.

"Platoon, at the lope."

Their speed increased dramatically. The pursuing Mexicans hesitated, then matched their pace.

The ground over which they raced was bounded on both sides by thick, almost impenetrable, thorny brush. It gradually narrowed to a place ahead where the open space between the brush was only ten yards wide. A shallow dry arroyo crossed there, providing an ideal defensive position.

"When we get to the arroyo, dismount and spread out five wide and four deep. The guidon bearer will hold the horses in the rear and I will get up the back side of the arroyo. Platoon, gallop!"

They charged ahead, dismounted, and took up defensive positions. The thick brush would prevent the Mexican cavalry from flanking them. The lancers depended entirely on the eight foot lances for offense, so they must be within a few feet of the Americans to attack. They stopped and evaluated the situation.

On order from their captain, the bugler sounded the charge. A hundred Mexican lancers and their officers galloped forward into the ever narrowing space.

At fifty yards, the American carbines fired by rank, one row after the other of carefully aimed shots. Sixteen lancers fell dead or wounded from their horses.

The charge faltered. They didn't advance, but didn't regroup. They seemed unsure of how to proceed. The Americans didn't suffer from indecision.

At twenty yards, Sergeant Branam put a bullet from his Walker through the head of the commanding captain. Adjusting his aim, he dropped a lieutenant and four enlisted men.

"Resume firing!"

As they did, the Mexicans raced to get away from the deadly fire of the Americans. Thirty-one men and officers would never fight again.

"Good job, men. Reload, then remount."

"Column of twos, long trot. Ho!"

They moved out and were met within a mile by reinforcements. The fresh troops swung in a wide arch to find the depleted Mexican cavalry crossing the Rio Grande back into Mexico. First blood of the war to come had been drawn. Much more would be spilled before peace would return.

───────────

On May 3, 1846, Mexican artillery opened fire from Matamoros on Fort Texas. The Americans returned fire. The cannon duel continued for a week. Two American soldiers were killed, including Major Brown. The fort was renamed Fort Brown in his honor.

On May 8, General Taylor marched to the relief of Fort Brown with twenty-four hundred American troops. Mexican General Arista avoided the guns of Fort Brown and intercepted Taylor's force at Palo Alto with thirty-four hundred troops.

Taylor employed a new tactic of "flying artillery." Whole batteries of four or more field cannon, usually twelve pounders or smaller, were each pulled by six strong horses. The cannon were quickly wheeled into place and unhitched. Aimed shots were fired at vulnerable places in the enemy defenses. Then, before the enemy could find the range, they galloped to another position. This kept the enemy off balance and gave the American infantry time to advance.

Arista's plan to over-power the Americans with superior numbers was disrupted by the completely unexpected flying artillery attack. The Mexicans retreated to regroup.

The next day the Mexicans held a good defensive position at Resaca de la Palma. The Americans attacked across a dry creek bed and captured much of the Mexican artillery. There was fierce hand to hand fighting resulting in a Mexican retreat. Their line of retreat placed Arista's soldiers well within the range of the cannon of Fort Brown. The guns tore into the Mexican right flank as the Americans battered the rear guard. The Mexicans suffered heavy casualties as they struggled back to Matamoros.

President Polk received word that hostilities had erupted on the border. On May 11, 1846, the United States declared war on Mexico.

———————

The American Navy quickly blockaded the Gulf and Pacific ports of Mexico. Reinforcements poured into Texas. Texas Rangers and militia companies were recruited as volunteers.

There was to be an attack on two fronts. First, an attack from the north would secure the scant Mexican forces in the rear of Taylor's army. These attacks were directed at Santa Fe and Albuquerque, and a few small scattered garrisons in Arizona. From there, they would proceed to California to secure the isolated Mexican forces. As this was accomplished, General Taylor would lead a large American force into north central Mexico to neutralize any threat to the border.

On the second front, General Winfield Scott would mount a large scale amphibious assault at Vera Cruz. Once Vera Cruz was secure, they would approach Mexico City from the east.

———————

I received a sealed letter from Sam Houston, who served as Senator from Texas in the Congress of the United States.

Lieutenant Colonel Aaron Turner
Commanding Officer, Northeast Texas Militia

My friend Aaron,

A special need has arisen which you are uniquely qualified to fulfill. You have direct first-hand knowledge of both the harbor and city fortresses in Vera Cruz. You are also fully fluent in Spanish, as are many of your regiment. I have been asked to offer you a promotion to Colonel of Scouts, United States Ranging Regiment. You would act as an aide to General Scott and command the Ranging companies of your regiment in scouting for the army.

You will be well supplied with horses and weapons. You will take as many men of your militia regiment as you can spare without opening your homes to undue danger from Comanche attacks.

If I am not mistaken, you are past sixty years old. This will be an arduous undertaking for a man of any age, and should you decline, I will understand completely. Your service to Texas has been far above and beyond the call of duty. Should you choose to accept, I have made unique arrangements to have you and every man in your command armed with a pair of the new Colt Walker .44 revolvers.

I have instructed the courier to wait for your response, as long as it takes.

I was saddened to learn of the tragic loss of our mutual friend and patriot, Captain Robert Contois. Both you and Captain Rob were loyal friends when I had but few.

Best personal regards,
Your friend and comrade in arms,

Sam Houston
United States Senator
Washington

I invited the courier detail of five cavalrymen to stable their horses with fresh hay, oats and water while I considered my response. This would require some thought and consultation with Nancy.

"Lieutenant Johnson, this is going to require some time. I would like to think about it over night. If you and your men are able to wait that long, we would be happy to have you as guests in our home."

"Sir, I was advised that this might take some time. My men and I would be delighted to accept your generous offer. It is not hard to convince a soldier to accept a real bed and home-cooked food."

————

Nancy fixed a good supper and seemed to enjoy watching the five young mendevouring her food. Needless to say, there were no leftovers.

"Ma'am, on behalf of my men and me, we thank you for such a wonderful meal."

"Glad you enjoyed it, gentlemen."

David was fascinated with the soldiers in their uniforms. They entertained him while I helped Nancy with the dishes.

"Well, what do you think?"

"They seem like nice young men."

"You know what I mean."

"Mexico? Take a wild guess what I think of a sixty-three year old man with a wife and child going off to fight in a foreign country."

"What shall I tell Sam Houston?"

"Aaron, here it is. I'm tired of you being gone off somewhere to fight somebody. I'd like to see an end to it. As much as I hate to see you go, it may put us closer to you finally staying home, because there won't be anybody left to fight. Tell him you'll go."

We spent the hours after our guests had gone to bed sitting on the upstairs gallery wrapped in one of the warm buffalo robes from our Wichita hunt. We didn't talk much, but watched the lightning bugs come out and listened to the night birds.

In the morning I signed my commission as Colonel of Scouts, Texas Volunteer Ranging Regiment. I was to hand-pick my own officers and men from my militia. Further orders would arrive later, but I was to arrive in Corpus Christi by February 1847. It had not occurred to me that it would be so far distant in time.

16

May, 1846, North central Mexico

GENERAL ZACHARY Taylor had divided his forces to accomplish various purposes. First was the Army of the West under General Stephen Kearney. They marched from Fort Leavenworth, Kansas, fifteen hundred strong. Santa Fe was taken without a shot being fired.

Kearney detached eight hundred men under Colonel Alexander Doniphan to secure Albuquerque, then sweep along the Rio Grande until they reinforced General Taylor. Kearney left a garrison to hold Santa Fe and headed west with the remainder of his force. He crossed the deserts of Arizona to reach California. He found that a small naval and marine force had already seized Monterey. His presence eliminated the token Mexican resistance and secured the United States claims to California.

The Army of Occupation under Taylor marched through the heart of northern Mexico. He commanded six thousand troops.

Mexican General Ampudia commanded seven thousand troops, but many of them were raw recruits. They waged a fighting retreat to Monterrey where they mounted a vigorous defense. After four days of determined fighting, a truce was declared on September 24, 1846. Taylor agreed to allow the Mexican army to retreat to Saltillo.

In the meantime, Santa Anna had been recalled from exile in Cuba. He arrived in San Luis Potosi to take command of an army of twenty-five thousand green recruits. The last chapter of our history with Santa Anna had yet to be written.

The Central Division under General Wool marched from San Antonio along the coastal road, scooping up small Mexican outposts before them. They turned inland and crossed the Chihuahuan desert to join Doniphan at Saltillo.

The armies were in place. Soon, there would be a clash of titans.

––––––––

I soon received a request from General Scott to review and make notations on the existing maps of the island fortress of San Juan de Ulua in the harbor of Vera Cruz and the two forts on the mainland. I was to hand deliver them to Corpus Christi. I worked on the maps from my memory of frequent visits there thirty years ago.

I selected Chance as my obvious choice for second in command. I asked Nick and Cody to go, as well as Tanner Moore, Logan and Gray. I knew I would need the services of Aaron Chavez and Angelo Lucio. The three Lane brothers from Louisiana Landing had proven handy in a fight, so I asked them to join us.

There was plenty of time to get in a good crop and get it harvested and stored. I was unsure how to proceed about my crop for the summer of 1847, as I knew it was unlikely we would be home that soon. Then I remembered the Adamson boys from Fort Parker.

I rode up one morning in December and made a proposal to them to work my farm for me. I offered them room and board, plus $20 a month, from spring planting until the cotton was picked. They jumped at the opportunity.

We received the promised Walker Colts and practiced with them until we could switch out cylinders on horseback and shoot with deadly accuracy. The guns were heavy with fierce recoil, but quite useful in experienced hands. We were also sent military carbines and cavalry sabers. Anticipating that none of us had used a saber, Lieutenant Johnson planned to instruct us in its proper use. This was not as easy as I had expected. There were special techniques to learn. We practiced charging at pumpkins set on poles and at Lieutenant Johnson who would take a defensive position on horseback with a saber or lance. Sometimes he was on foot with a musket and bayonet or an eight foot pike. The lances and pikes proved the hardest to learn to attack with a saber, but it could be done. We drilled until we were tired of looking at our horses.

"Colonel, if one of them Mexicans is coming at me with a lance, don't it make more sense just to shoot the son of a gun and just forget this saber business?"

"Cody, you need to know how to use that saber in case you get caught with an unloaded gun. It's not my first choice either."

We each selected two of our best Thoroughbred cross geldings for the trip. The army would pay us for them when we got to Corpus Christi.

In January our uniforms arrived with orders to arrive in Corpus Christi no later than February 15. The scout company uniforms were different than the regular United States cavalry. We were issued a buff colored wool coat, heavy weight white cotton shirts and blue cotton pants. We were issued campaign hats, which were broad brimmed, much like what we were accustomed to wearing, with a strap to fit under the chin to keep them in place.

The hats had a brass insignia in the front, similar to the one on our belts. We were allowed to select our own footwear from sturdy brogans, laced boots or cavalry boots. We each elected the high top boots we wore every day.

The epaulettes on my shoulders indicated the rank of full colonel. Chance wore the insignia of a major. Cody and Nick received captain's bars; all three of the Lane brothers received the insignias of lieutenants.

Lieutenant Johnson was promoted to First Lieutenant and assigned to my staff. Gray, Tanner, Logan, Chavez and Lucio were privates. Many additional men would be assigned to me on reaching Corpus Christi.

———————

Ten of us, in old clothes and fully armed, assembled before daylight on February 1, 1847, for the long ride. We would each lead a spare horse which would carry a pack saddle of supplies. We would pick up the Lane brothers on our way through Louisiana Landing. The other wives stood with Nancy on the porch in the misty gray light and said their goodbyes. This was the hardest parting I had known in my married life.

"I promise I'll be back. There is decent postal service for the military, so I'll write and hope you will, too." I held her and was reluctant to turn her loose. David, now five years old, pulled at my uniform sleeve.

"I love you, Daddy. Please come home."

"I picked him up and clung tightly to him. "I will, son, I will. Be good to your Mama while I'm gone."

We mounted up just as the sun appeared through the mists in the eastern sky. The Navasota was low, so we rode the horses across and followed the Camino Real once again.

We spent the night with the Applewhite family. In the morning the Lane brothers joined us. We took the ferry across the Brazos and followed the road as it angled away to the southwest and San Antonio.

We crossed the Colorado and camped where we had stayed so many years ago on our first trip to Texas. The ghosts of the past were with us every step of our journey.

We came to the adobe hacienda of Don Fernando de Zavala. It was abandoned. The tile roof was still in good repair, but the adobe walls were beginning to crumble. The large oak doors hung open. Cattle had apparently wandered through the once fine home, and a family of javalina about scared us to death as they tried to escape around us out the doors. The adobe corrals were still usable. The well there had not gone dry. We used a new rope and bucket to draw water for ourselves and the horses. We fed the horses some well deserved oats. We camped inside a barn adjacent to the corrals. The house was too fouled to use.

The next morning we let the horses graze a while in the unused pasture near the corrals. We had pushed them hard and still had a long way to go. We were on the road by mid-morning and arrived in San Antonio by late afternoon.

———————

The dusty city had not grown any more attractive to me since I was last there in the siege of 1836. It was hot, dusty and singularly unattractive.

The army maintained a headquarters building where the ever handy Lieutenant Johnson directed me. A Major Wardlow commanded here. Lieutenant Johnson politely requested that I be allowed to see the major.

A quarrelsome voice bellowed through the open door. "I don't have time to talk to any more country bumpkin militia officers. Let the quartermaster tell him where to billet."

We took our horses to the stables and were shown to shabby dirt floored tents for our lodgings. Lieutenant Johnson was obviously bothered.

"Sir, this isn't right. These tents are for enlisted men in transit. They're the worst accommodations on the post."

"I rather suspect you're right, Johnson. What are you thinking?"

"Sir, you, Major Chance and I should wash up and change

into our dress uniforms, then revisit the Major."

Soon we were all washed and dressed in our finest freshly brushed dress uniforms, with our sabers at our sides. Our second entry into the commander's office was less polite.

Johnson preceded us into the office. He snapped to attention and bellowed, "Ten Hut!" The young aide nearly fell out of his chair trying to rise to attention.

I gave a curt salute. "Who is in command here, Lieutenant?"

"I am by thunder!" bellowed the angry voice of the major as he barreled out of his office, putting on his jacket. "Who the hell wants to know?"

"You will address me as Colonel Turner, United States Army. Is this how you address a superior officer? Button that jacket! You are at attention."

His eyes bugged out and his jaw dropped open. "I, er, um, ahem. I beg the Colonel's pardon, sir."

"This is not my first visit to your office, Major. When I was announced earlier I believe you said you didn't have time to see any country bumpkin militia officers. Major Chance, Lieutenant Johnson, you were both present. Is my memory correct?"

"Yes, Colonel Turner. It is, sir. I shall address it in my report to General Scott, sir."

"Major Wardlow, you will have suitable quarters made available for my entire escort immediately. You will have our horses groomed, watered, and fed fresh hay and oats. The saddles are to be cleaned. Am I clear, Major Wardlow?" He gulped and nodded his head.

"Well jump to it, man!" The three of us shared a smile as the red faced major rushed out shouting orders.

Once he left, I asked the horrified young aide if he had any orders for me from General Scott. I was handed a clean, freshly sealed packet. I tore open the seal and read the orders.

"We'll be leaving in the morning on the road to Corpus Christi. What is your name, young man?"

"Smith, sir."

"Thank you for your help, Lieutenant Smith. I do not eat junior officers, only arrogant commanders."

———————

The road followed the Atascosa River until it merged into the Nueces. At that point, the old military road followed the Nueces the rest of the way to Corpus Christi. We were on the threshold of an odyssey we would never forget.

17

February 15, 1847, United States Army
headquarters, Corpus Christi, Texas

CORPUS CHRISTI WAS beautiful in the mild winter breezes from the Gulf of Mexico. An immense military camp spread out north of town. The tents were precisely laid out in rows, back to back, with a "street" separating the next double row.

Men and horses were everywhere. There was a large artillery park where the cannon and their caissons were placed in perfect order.

The harbor was full of ships. There were steam frigates armed with large cannon, armed sailing sloops, and huge transport ships. There were oddly built ships that only carried one gun in the center of a low deck. These were the "bomb ketches," armed only with one enormous mortar. These mortars could throw one hundred pound exploding shells high into the air over enemy defenses and rain down death and destruction from the sky.

Our unit was designated United States Army, Corp of Scouts, First Regiment, Companies A and B. I had been assigned two full companies to augment my own small group. Company A included the same platoon which had precipitated the war, under the guidance of Sergeant Stan Branam.

Our small regiment was assigned a place within

the great camp. The men soon had the large tents assembled, our gear stowed, and the horses tended.

My regiment was a detached command, to answer directly to General Scott and his staff. Company A was placed under the command of Captain Cody Teel, now nearing forty years old. Tanner Lane and his brother, Tyler, were the two second lieutenants. First Sergeant Branam led First Platoon, which included Gray, Logan and Tanner Moore.

Company B was commanded by Nick Teel, First Lieutenant Johnson, and Second Lieutenant Blake Lane. Both companies were fleshed out with veteran soldiers.

Chance, as major, was my second in command and strong right arm. The men, even the new ones, respected him. It would be awkward for some of them to call him anything other than Chance. It wasn't an issue with us, but for the sake of appearance, we would work on it. Chavez and Lucio would be our couriers. They did not know it yet, but they would have far more important and dangerous duties.

The whole regiment had been outfitted with a pair of Walker Colt .44s, .50 carbines and sabers. As promised, we would be very well mounted.

––––––––––

Chance and I met with General Scott or his staff every day. They had carefully reviewed my notes about the fortifications at Vera Cruz. Of course, they had current information to add to mine about troop dispositions and gun placements. The naval officers calculated the best use of their flat shooting naval guns and the high arching shots of their huge mortars.

They were especially interested in the two forts in the city of Vera Cruz. The plan was to land the army, cavalry and artillery south of Vera Cruz and to envelop the city from the west. The navy would bombard the harbor fortress and both city garrisons.

"Colonel Turner, you and your scouts must make certain that

we are not surprised by a Mexican field army or relief force sent to support Vera Cruz. If you fail to detect the presence of an enemy force of even moderate strength, this whole operation could become a disaster. Senator Houston assures me you are the man for the job." General Scott was red-faced with seriousness as he addressed me. His whole staff had their eyes riveted on me, the unknown old man from Texas.

"I understand, sir." What was I doing here? Thousands of lives depended on the job done by me and my men.

————————

News poured in that on February 22 and 23 the Americans had engaged a numerically superior Mexican force at a place call Buena Vista. The "Napoleon of the West," Santa Anna, had left San Luis Potosi with twenty-five thousand men. By that time the army of conscripted peasants had been reduced to fifteen thousand by mass desertions.

Santa Anna deployed his troops across a huge front blocking the smaller American army's only route to Mexico City. He had chosen the ground so that he could use his highly trained lancers to flank the Americans. He had assembled a large collection of artillery, including heavy twenty-four pound guns, in the center of his position.

General Taylor had consolidated his forces and had received a modest reinforcement. He now commanded four thousand five hundred men. He deployed his men in a mountain pass known as Buena Vista facing Santa Anna's fifteen thousand. The mountains would prevent a flanking maneuver by the Mexican cavalry, and any assault on the American position would have to be made up hill.

On February 22, Santa Anna sent envoys to demand the Americans surrender. Zachary Taylor declined in terms that could not be misunderstood. The Americans had come to fight, not talk.

The next morning began with a terrible thundering as the whole Mexican artillery park opened fire on the American position. Santa Anna then sent a large body of infantry up the steep slope against the American left flank. They valiantly repelled assault after assault at huge cost in Mexican lives, but the weight of their overwhelming numerical superiority slowly drove the American left back.

Taylor employed a dangerous tactic. He divided his force in the presence of a superior enemy. He sent the Mississippi Rifle Regiment under Colonel Jefferson Davis behind the battered left flank and out onto the slope to attack the exposed right flank of the attacking Mexican infantry.

The Mississippi Rifles poured a hot and deadly fire into the Mexican flank. The chaos created by the unexpected attack gave the injured American line time to fall back. They reformed into an angled line between the American center and the rocky mountain side. The ruins of an abandoned hacienda provided a bastion to anchor the middle of the new left flank. A fresh artillery battery was sent to reinforce the left, pouring canister and grape shot into the disrupted Mexican attackers. The Third Indiana Regiment of Infantry slipped behind the new line and reinforced Davis and his Mississippians. The momentum of the attack had turned. The Mexicans retreated with heavy losses.

Santa Anna once again turned to his heavy artillery for a concentrated assault on the American center. Under the cover of artillery for part of the way, a fresh Mexican assault led by General Perez was launched against the American center.

Captain Braxton Bragg commanded the American artillery in the center. At a distance, Bragg's guns disrupted the Mexican attack with solid shot. As the enemy drew closer, the gunners began firing grape shot into the concentrated Mexican forces. The one pound iron shot tore ragged holes in the Mexican lines. Finally, as they closed to within a hundred yards, the Americans opened fire with deadly canister. Each shot unleashed hundreds of half inch musket balls that turned the Mexican lines into blood and gore.

The Mexican attack stalled. The American rifles added their contribution to the work of the cannon. Mexican soldiers were falling like over-ripe apples in a high wind. They attempted an orderly retreat, but the soldiers wanted to get away from the deadly cannon. The soldiers' valor spent, they broke and ran down the rocky slope.

The Americans stood to their guns through the night, expecting a renewed attack in the morning. However, the rising sun revealed that the much larger Mexican force had abandoned their position.

Santa Anna retreated to Mexico City. He deposed the president and declared himself dictator. He marshaled his forces and headed east to try to stop the approach of General Scott.

18

March 1, 1847, United States Army Headquarters, Corpus Christi, Texas

WE WERE GIVEN EXPLICIT orders on which men, materials and horses went into which transports in a specific order. My scout regiment was loaded aboard two side-wheeler transports. The ships had been especially modified to handle horses. In addition to the single starboard side-wheel, the ships also carried a full set of sails.

As the large squadron of ships left Corpus Christi and steamed beyond the protection of the barrier islands, a southerly breeze raised a steady chop. I was excited to be at sea again after so many years. I had always loved the sea. The heavily loaded transports took the increasing waves with all the grace of a fat cow jumping a fence. The bow rose up and plunged down. I noticed many of my men with their heads over the railing.

"Chance, it looks like the sea doesn't agree with you."

"No, sir." His face was ashen as he gripped the railing. I had never seen Chance where he wasn't in total control of any situation.

Cody was in the ship's bow holding on to the

rigging allowing the salt spray to soak his old clothes. "Colonel, this is like ridin' a rank horse. I like it!" I left him to enjoy his pleasure. I was getting wet.

As the day wore on, the wind laid and the water was almost smooth. The railings were now free of sick soldiers and replaced by a few who seemed to enjoy the view.

The wind turned fair for the use of the sails, so the flotilla proceeded under steam and sail over calm waters. We sailed past Vera Cruz far enough out to sea that the fleet would not be seen.

The ships were divided into two groups. The largest group included the transports and special landing boats accompanied by a few warships. The smaller group contained the heavily armed frigates and bomb ketches.

On March 9, 1847, the attack fleet stood beyond the horizon off of Vera Cruz. The transport fleet anchored a few miles south of Vera Cruz as close in as they could get to Collado Beach. The area had been selected for the unloading and landing of horses, men and materials.

A special Marine detachment went ashore first. They fanned out into skirmish lines and swept the area for the presence of Mexican troops. Finding none, they fired a rocket to signal that it was clear for the second wave to land. They reinforced the skirmish lines and prepared to assist the steadily arriving boats.

My scouts were in the next group sent ashore. The horses were fitted into special slings, and their heads were covered to keep them calm. They were raised over the side and carefully lowered into flat bottomed landing boats. Once they were as close to shore as possible, they were led out into knee deep water by waiting Marines who escorted them onto the gently sloping beach.

The saddled horses were secured on shore. My men climbed into landing boats that held about twenty men each. They entered the boats by platoons. The odd looking craft were able to get close to the beach, dropping us in water that was not over boot-top deep.

We found our individual mounts and kept the men together with their platoon leaders to avoid confusion. Sergeant Branam had First Platoon, A Company, which included the younger men from home.

"Alright, men. Keep your holsters over your shoulders and your rifle out of the water. Find your horse, check the bridle and the cinches.

"Good. Throw your saddle holsters over the horn like you've been taught. Stand at the ready."

The other sergeants in both companies similarly prepared their platoons and reported to their lieutenants. The lieutenants passed their readiness along the chain of command to Major Chance. Chavez and Lucio were at our sides to assist in whatever needed doing.

"Alright, Chance. Give the order."

"Captains, prepare your companies to mount. Mount!"

As soon as the companies had mounted they fanned out in predetermined directions to scout far ahead of the Marine skirmish lines. The platoon leaders were not to engage any enemy encountered, but immediately have their bugler sound recall and return to the beach.

After the longest half hour of my life, the platoons sent riders back to inform me they had found no enemy soldiers. I breathed a sigh of relief.

"Chance, send those men back to their platoons. They are to stand by for orders."

The horsemen galloped away. Chance had Chavez light a white rocket to signal the waiting ships the area was secure. The rocket flared up, burst with a deafening boom and a bright white light.

Hundreds of landing craft appeared all along the beach as they were rowed ashore with platoons of men. A waiting sloop had sailed away to alert the battle fleet the landing was under way. By midnight, General Scott and his entire army were on the shore.

Only the heavy cannon had yet to be unloaded. We would proceed according to plan without them.

As the infantry landed, my scout regiment was released for reconnaissance farther out. Two platoons of B Company rode south along the coast, while the other platoons probed to the southwest and west. Nothing more than a few small farmer's huts and goats were found.

Company A probed northwest and north. First Platoon under Sergeant Branam spotted a Mexican cavalry patrol. He kept his platoon in visual contact with them, as he sent riders to alert the other platoons of the enemy's presence, and a rider to notify me.

A smiling eager young Private Gray Jamison reined up in front of me.

"Reverend Turner, I mean Colonel Turner! There's Mexican cavalry ahead!"

"Private Jamison, please report through the proper chain of command to Major Chance."

"Yes, sir. Major Chance. Private Jamison, Company A, First Platoon reporting, sir."

Grinning at both of us, Chance avoided laughing out loud. "Yes, private?"

"Sergeant Branam's compliments, sir. We have found a body of Mexican cavalry, sir."

"How many, private?"

"Heck if I know, Chance. Oops. Sorry, sir. Sergeant Branam reports a full company of dragoons, sir."

"Well done, private. Your orders, Colonel?"

"Send Lucio to find Colonel Harney with the American dragoons and make him aware of the presence of Mexican cavalry. Have Private Jamison wait here until Colonel Harney's regiment arrives. He is to personally guide them back to his platoon."

"Gray, good job, son!"

Within minutes, we could hear the approach of cavalry. Three companies of dragoons arrived under the personal command of Colonel Harney.

"Colonel Turner, would you kindly have one of your scouts direct us?"

"Of course, Colonel. Private Jamison, you are to guide the colonel's regiment."

"Yes sir, Colonel Turner. Colonel Harney?"

"Regiment, at the long trot. Ho!"

The regiment overwhelmed the Mexican dragoons in a brief fight. My scouts were again sent farther out. They reported the location of the main aquaduct into Vera Cruz. A company of heavy infantry accompanied by a team of engineers stopped the flow of water into the sleeping city.

The main army was slowly enveloping the city. By daylight they were almost into position.

The coming of the dawn revealed the presence of our forces to the surprised Mexican sentries. Bells rang, bugles sounded. Soon a few random cannon fired from the walls of the garrison, as much to alert the city as to do any damage.

As the first Mexican cannon fired, it was no longer necessary to conceal our presence. An exploding white rocket spiraled upward from each brigade indicating their unit was in place and ready to fight. The American battle fleet appeared on the horizon with the rising sun behind it.

The Mexican army launched several sorties against the American positions. They were easily repelled. The heavy artillery would not be in position for a few days.

By March 22, all was in place to begin the massive bombardment of the thirsty city. The Mexican commander, General Juan Morales, declined to surrender. An artillery battery of the heaviest siege guns had been carefully placed under the direction of Captain Robert E. Lee. The great guns opened fire on the surrounded city.

The heavy naval guns and mortars joined the fight. The mortars were a sight to behold. The massive shells could be seen rising up until they reached their highest point, then plunging down into the crumbling city with a tremendous explosion. The effect of the combined bombardment was devastating. Military and civilian casualties began to mount. My scouts detected the approach of the advance guard of a relief column of approximately two thousand Mexican infantry and several cannon.

Colonel Harney's regiment of dragoons and the Third Infantry Division quickly defeated the relief column. After three days of continuous bombardment, with no relief in sight, the city and its fortresses surrendered. The east coast of Mexico was now open for American supplies and reinforcements.

19

April 18, 1847, Cerro Gordo, Jalapa, Mexico

WE HAD SECURED VERA Cruz. The port swelled with men and war materials. A strong garrison force was left to defend the city, which also remained under the vigilance of the warships along the coast and in the harbor.

Our Ranging Regiment, or scouts, depending on who you asked, had been sent ahead of the main column as it rolled westward toward distant Mexico City. We discovered advance elements of Santa Anna's main force near the city of Jalapa at a place called Cerro Gordo, which translated as "fat mountain."

I sent Company A to the south and Company B to the north to scout. They were able to give a detailed description of the disposition of the Mexican army, estimated at nine to ten thousand men, plus cavalry and artillery.

Chance and I rode back to report to General Scott. He ordered to us try to locate a weak spot in the Mexican position.

On returning, we sent our platoons out to prowl near the Mexican positions. Nick discovered what he believed to be just such a weakness. Chance and I followed him there to see for ourselves.

There was a rocky knoll at the extreme north end of the Mexican line. It was only lightly defended. If this position could be taken, artillery could be manhandled into position. The guns would be able to sweep the length of the Mexican line, which stretched from north to south.

The information was given to General Scott. On conferring with his staff, it was decided that two of the three American divisions would prepare to make a frontal assault from the east, just at the extreme range of the Mexican artillery. The Third Division would capture the knoll and reinforce it with artillery and enough troops to repel any counter attack. The remainder of the division was to proceed around the knoll and prepare to hit the Mexican left flank as soon as the frontal diversion was launched. The scout regiment was to swing even farther west and disrupt or capture the Mexican supply lines and baggage train. If the opportunity presented, we were to attack the Mexican line from the rear when the Third Division was attacking from the north.

_____

In the pre-dawn haze of April 18, 1847, two full American divisions assembled to make a frontal assault by columns against the Mexican army situated along the heights of Cerro Gordo. As daylight approached, the Mexican forces had the sun full in their faces. Still they could see a large army preparing to attack.

What they failed to see was another American division concealed from sight on their left flank. Cannon flashed across the front of the army assembled in their front, drawing all attention there.

As they fired, American infantry overran the rocky hill at the north end of the Mexican line. Horses hauled the heavy twelve pounder field cannon as close as they could to the knoll. The engineers and infantry manhandled the guns into place. They had a full sweep of the Mexican line.

An entire brigade was left to defend the hill from a counter-attack as the guns spewed forth destruction on the unsuspecting Mexican line. The rest of the division poured around the hill hitting the Mexicans in their extreme left flank.

Santa Anna swung his northern most brigades to stop the American onslaught. A sharp battle quickly developed.

Our regiment made a wide loop and fell upon the Mexican baggage train in the rear. The few guards and freighters fled for their lives. We found ourselves about four hundred yards in the rear of the Mexican line.

I ordered an officers' call. "This is a dangerous situation. We'll trot in with a full two company front to within one hundred yards of the Mexican line and halt. The men are to take one well aimed shot with their carbines. The bugler will sound the charge. Once we are within fifty yards, the men are to draw their revolvers and close the range. We do not want to get too close to those bayonets. At fifty feet, the men are to swing north and head for the safety of the American line that is attacking the Mexicans there. They are to reform by company and reload everything they own. Questions?"

There were serious looks on their faces, but no questions. "Let's go get 'em. God bless Texas!"

The men formed a two company front stretching from north to south; two hundred hardened men armed to the teeth, with no love for their enemy. Cody would lead Company A on the north, and Nick would lead Company B on the south. Major Chance, Lucio, and Chavez and I would remain behind the main line.

"Companies forward at the trot." At a hundred yards from the Mexican line I ordered a halt. "One well aimed shot with your carbines. When the bugles sound, you will sheath your rifles, draw your pistols and charge. When you are within fifty yards you may fire at will. Buglers will sound recall and the regiment will break off the engagement and ride north to the American line and reassemble there."

"Regiment, ready. Aim. Fire!"

Chavez and Lucio sounded the charge and the line galloped

forward. In the confusion of the battle the shots we had fired couldn't be distinguished from the others. We were not discovered until it was too late. At fifty yards, two hundred angry Texans took their revenge for years of mistreatment by the Mexicans, and the memories of the Alamo and Goliad still ringing in their minds. The fact that each man was able to fire twelve deadly shots greatly multiplied the firepower directed at the Mexican rear.

Mexicans soldiers fell like ripe grain before the scythe. The raw Mexican troops saw Americans to the north, the east and the west. Many threw down their weapons and ran hard to the south, straight into the center of their own line. The left flank of the Mexican army crumbled. The Third division swept down on the fleeing remnants and assaulted the chaos in the center of the Mexican line. The center disintegrated and the Mexicans were routed.

Santa Anna was seen fleeing the field on horseback so quickly that he lost his wooden leg. It was found by the men of the Iowa Forth Regiment who took it home for a war souvenir.

The Americans had lost sixty-three dead, and three hundred sixty-seven wounded. The Mexicans had four hundred thirty-six dead, seven hundred sixty-four wounded and three thousand captured. It was an overwhelming victory. The road to Mexico City lay open before us.

20

August, 1847, outside Mexico City

IT WAS AN EERIE FEELING as we camped near Mexico City. The land itself had an ancient, foreign feel. Smoking volcanoes could be seen on the skyline. We knew an enemy of size and determination lay somewhere within the ring of smoking mountains.

We had a special job for Aaron Chavez and Angelo Lucio. They were to be our spies.

We bought four rather plain burros from a local farmer. The boys fitted themselves out in peasant clothes. They wore tattered white cotton shirts and pants. Second hand sandals and well-worn sombreros completed the outfit. They carefully rehearsed their stories of who they were, where they came from and where they were going.

Two of the burros were loaded with cut brush wood for cooking fires. They would ride the other burros bareback, carrying morrals of parched corn, beans, corn tortillas and a gourd of water. They carried no weapons, not even a poor man's knife.

For the most part they were unnoticed by anyone. As they approached from the east, they noticed two heavily fortified positions of Mexican heavy artillery commanding the eastern entrance to the Valley of Mexico.

Riding on closer to the city they were challenged at a road block. Their stories were well rehearsed and well played. Aaron was the spokesman. He explained they were bringing wood to sell at the market so they could buy seed corn. His mentally slow cousin had fed theirs to the chickens. When Angelo was questioned he mumbled, "Angelo, si. Buenas dias. Angelo, si? Buenas dias." The guards shook their heads and laughed.

Aaron asked them if there was a good road to take to the south because he wanted to visit an uncle there, but he had never come to Mexico City before and didn't know the way. They happily obliged him by describing the road that would take them between the lakes, then across a bad area of black rocks. If they followed it for it a few days, they would come to his uncle's village.

He thanked them and Angelo added, "Angelo, adios, si?" The soldiers just laughed and waved good bye.

The burros clipped along at a slow trot as they explored as much of Mexico City as they could see. They were amazed by the size and grandeur of parts of the sprawling city. The Castle of Chapultepec was a fortress and military school on the west side of the great city. It was well defended.

As they turned south, they passed Molino del Rey, the King's Mill, which was a gunpowder factory and foundry for weapons. The road wound past an old walled convent, Santa Maria de Churubusco, which had been heavily garrisoned.

Something else there startled them. There were Mexican soldiers speaking English! On closer observation they discovered these were mostly American deserters of Irish descent who had abandoned Taylor's army in the north. They had been formed into La Brigada de San Patrico, the Brigade of Saint Patrick.

The work done by Chavez and Lucio resulted in a significant change of the plan of attack. General Scott sent his army to the southwest, by-passing the troubling defenses on the eastern approaches to the city.

Santa Anna responded by shifting troops to cover the southern approaches, but lost the advantage of his heavy artillery emplacements. It would take too long to move the huge guns to meet the changing threat.

The American army enjoyed success as it pushed back the advance elements of the Mexican army in the south. It became much harder when we reached the fortified position at Churubusco.

On August 20, 1847, five miles south of the capital, lay the village of Churubusco; the Americans had their hands full. The Mexican army had centered its defenses around the stone walls of the Franciscan convent of Santa Maria de Churubusco. A small river, crossed by only one small bridge, formed a natural defensive barrier in front of the convent and the flanking infantry lines. The Mexicans had added a series of trenches to bolster their defenses. The position had been reinforced by troops fleeing the two earlier defeats.

The Americans began their offensive by sending a brigade of infantry to assault the troops on the Mexican right flank. The flank crumbled with the loss of five cannon and five hundred taken prisoner. The Mexicans adjusted their lines and fought with a will.

The Americans launched a frontal assault of five thousand men directly at the Mexican center and the convent. Thirty-eight hundred Mexicans with seven cannon repelled the American attack. They never made it across the river.

General Scott shifted the attack to the Mexican left flank, which was particularly well entrenched. The Mexicans narrowly repelled the attack.

A second American attack on the center focused on seizing the bridge. Although the river was not large, the banks were steep and difficult to cross. The troops crossing the river were exposed to lethal musket fire at close range. The bridge was almost in American hands when three small companies of Mexican provincial militia reinforced the weakening defenses. They continued to hold the bridge until they ran out of ammunition. The Mexican army used a wide variety of calibers in their muskets. The paper cartridges that arrived for them were useless to the men defending the bridge. The remaining Mexican troops launched a desperate bayonet charge across the bridge, only to be cut down by American rifles. All that remained of the Mexican defenses was the stone convent and stubs of their right and left flanks.

Aaron Chavez galloped up. "Colonel Turner! It's them. The Brigada San Patricio. I saw the green emblem on their coats!"

I sent Chance at a gallop to report to General Scott. "General Scott, Major Chance, Ranging Regiment, reporting from Colonel Turner, sir."

"Can't you see I'm busy? State your business and be quick about it."

"Sir, our scouts report the convent is being defended by the San Patricios along with Mexican troops."

"Those Irish deserters! No wonder they are fighting so hard. You tell Colonel Turner I want every surviving San Patricio brought to me personally as soon as the convent falls. I'll hang every one of them."

The cannon defending the convent finally overheated and exploded or were taken out of action by our artillery. A brigade commanded by Colonel Franklin Pierce successfully secured the bridge. American troops poured across the river, forcing the remaining Mexican troops from the center inside the convent. On the remnant of the Mexican right flank, General Shield's men swept the surviving troops away from the walls of the convent.

My regiment was ordered to support General Worth's division as they attempted to dislodge the remnants of the Mexican left flank entrenched near the convent's walls. Worth's infantry engaged the enemy from across the bend of the river that wrapped around the convent's east side.

I led my regiment behind the screen provided by Worth's offensive. Once we were north of the Mexican position, we were able to ford the river on horseback.

We quickly regrouped. "Company A, platoon front. Sweep

everything between the river and the trenches. Company B, platoon front. Get between the trenches and the convent walls."

The companies formed up, twenty men wide and five men deep. Once they were in position, I gave the order they had expected. "Bugler, sound the charge!"

The piercing bugle notes added to the noise of battle as two hundred mounted men surged forward at the gallop. The Mexicans heard the bugles and crashing hooves. They realized they had been out flanked.

The two companies broke through the Mexican position, Colts blazing death in every direction. As they passed beneath the walls of the convent, muskets fired into Company B. Lieutenant Blake Lane was shot from his horse, dead where he fell.

The regiment had accomplished their mission. The troops outside the convent were dead or captured. The bugler sounded recall. The men galloped back to the north.

Lieutenants Tanner and Tyler Lane stayed behind. Tanner dismounted, while Tyler used his horse to shield his fallen brother. His pistols kept the Mexicans in the convent from getting too brave. Musket fire erupted from along the walls as Tanner hoisted his brother's dead body in front of his saddle. The horse shied from the smell of blood, but Tanner managed to get on. Tanner passed Blake's pistols to Tyler to try to keep the Mexicans occupied. As soon as he was in the saddle they galloped for the safety of our line.

A final rattle of musket fire caused Tyler's horse to stumble, but he regained his footing and safely reached our ranks. A musket ball had hit the horse in the lungs. He collapsed and died as Tyler dismounted.

————————

There were many defenders still packed in the convent. They fought desperately for another three hours, even though their position was hopeless. As their rate of fire dropped to a sputter, a white flag appeared above the convent walls. They had not run out of fight, they had run out of ammunition.

The Battle of Churubusco had ended with a costly American victory. The American force of eight thousand five hundred had lost one hundred and thirty-nine dead and a staggering eight hundred and sixty-five wounded. The Mexicans had lost two hundred and sixty-three dead, four hundred and sixty wounded, and one thousand two hundred and sixty-one captured. This included seventy-two American deserters from among the San Patricios.

These unfortunate men had not only deserted, but had turned their guns against their comrades at arms. This was clearly treason. My regiment sorted these men away from the other captives and herded them directly to General Scott.

21

September 6, 1847, Molino del Rey, Mexico City

AFTER THE POUNDING taken by both armies at Churubusco, an armistice was negotiated and surrender talks began. However, reinforcements from other parts of Mexico were finding their way to the capital. My scouts reported a heavy concentration of troops at Molino del Rey.

My scouts estimated there were around four thousand troops in position at the mill, plus they had counted forty pieces of artillery. The fortifications were only a thousand yards from Chapultepec Castle, the last obstacle to the gates of the great city. General Scott ordered General Worth to attack and destroy the powder mill and armory.

Mexican reserve forces were scattered in the forest between the mill and Chapultepec, which itself was heavily defended. In all, Santa Anna not only commanded the four thousand men at the mill, but a total of fourteen thousand troops that day. General Worth, believing he was attacking only four thousand men, began the assault with two thousand eight hundred.

The American heavy artillery had been situated well in range of the powder mill. The big guns opened fire and did not stop. The Mexicans defending the mill appeared shaken. At the moment the artillery barrage stopped, American troops rushed in to take advantage of the breaches in the defenses the cannon had caused.

Mexican field artillery was quickly wheeled into position to rake the American advance forces in the flank. Mexican soldiers appeared by the hundreds firing from the roof of the stone buildings. Although the Americans suffered heavy casualties, they were quickly reinforced and managed to hold on to their position in the breach in the enemy line.

An American field battery was wheeled into place on the right, even though this placed them within the range of Chapultepec's guns. On the left, an American assault was driven back with heavy losses. Even though the infantry failed, the artillery soon made the Mexican left flank abandon their position. With the collapse of both the right and left flank, and the Americans occupying a gaping hole in the center of their line, the Mexicans fell back to Chapultepec. The Americans had lost eight hundred men. The Mexicans had suffered eight hundred casualties and eight hundred and fifty captured. It had been another costly American victory.

———

Desperately needed reinforcements and supplies arrived from the coast, bringing General Scott's force up to thirteen thousand well supplied soldiers. My force had played only a minor role at Molino del Rey and had recovered from the hard fighting at Churubusco.

The next objective was Chapultepec Castle. The fortress stood atop a two hundred foot hill. The sides of the hill were extremely steep except on the south where the slope was manageable.

The fortress itself contained several hundred men, plus two hundred teenaged cadets of the military school. Another four thousand soldiers guarded the approaches to the fortress.

The American artillery carefully placed their heaviest guns to direct fire at the fortress itself. Lighter guns were situated where they could work misery on the troops at the base of the hill. Two storming parties of light infantry of two hundred and fifty men each would attack the castle. One group would assault the relatively gentle southern slope, while the other would attempt a steep climb up the southeastern face of the hill.

At dawn on September 12, 1847, a massive artillery barrage began that did not stop until dark. The valley between the artillery and Chapultepec was so thick with smoke the Mexican soldiers coughed and could barely see because of the burning of their eyes.

At daylight the following morning the artillery attack was renewed. When the guns fell silent at eight in the morning, the Mexican position was attacked by American infantry. Besides the storming parties, a full brigade formed the center of the American attack. On the American left were two regiments of infantry, and on the right was a collection of eight companies under Lieutenant Colonel Joseph E. Johnston.

The Americans were able to drive most of the Mexican forces away from the base of the hill, but the attack stalled until storming ladders could be sent forward from the rear. Major George Pickett was the first American to reach the top of the walls with ladders. More men swarmed up the ladders until a firm foothold had been established at the top, inside the doomed fortress.

A strong Mexican counter attack at the base of the hill threatened the whole operation. A young Lieutenant Thomas J. Jackson commanded a battery of field artillery, which delivered such a deadly storm of cannon fire the Mexicans were mowed down like ripe wheat. American infantry succeeded in driving the survivors from the field.

With Americans already inside the castle walls, General Nicolas Bravo had to divert men from the defense of the south slope. The shift in troops allowed the attackers to successfully enter the fortress at the top of the slope. American reinforcements poured like a river into the castle.

Caught between the two fronts, General Bravo, commander of the fortress surrendered. However, six cadets refused to surrender and fought to their death. The last cadet wrapped himself in the Mexican flag and threw himself over the wall two hundred feet to his death.

At the moment the American flag was raised over Chapultepec, the San Patricios were all hanged in full sight of the hill.

The fortress was ours at a cost of eight hundred and sixty-two American casualties. The Mexicans suffered eighteen hundred killed or wounded and eight hundred and twenty-three captured. Once again, American and Mexican blood stained the soil of Mexico.

_____

The victory was pressed to the very edge of the city. A garrison force secured the castle, while a force under General Quitman attacked the Belen Gate. A second force under General Worth attacked the San Cosme Gate. Our regiment was assigned to support General Worth.

The Belen Gate attack had been intended to only be a feint to draw troops away from the primary objective, the San Cosme Gate. However, it quickly escalated into a major engagement with reinforcements from both armies. As more and more American troops joined the attack, the Mexican defense collapsed.

To the north, Captain Robert E. Lee led the attack on the San Cosme Gate. A force of fifteen hundred Mexican cavalry hit the advancing Americans in the left flank. The infantry wheeled to face the attack. My regiment was sent west in a race to flank the enemy.

My two hundred men successfully reached a position to the west of the Mexican cavalry.

"Company B, assume company front position. Company A, assume company position in the second rank. On my order, the regiment will advance. Front rank will direct aimed carbine fire at the enemy at one hundred yards. Company A will assume the position of front rank and offer aimed carbine fire. We will then attack at the long trot. On my orders you will engage the enemy with your pistols."

"Regiment, advance." We trotted to within a hundred yards of the enemy. "Front rank, aim, fire! Second rank, advance to front.

Ready, aim, fire!" Two Mexican companies wheeled to face us.

"Regiment, at the long trot. Charge!" We closed to within fifty feet. "Fire!"

With our horses covering the ground at a long trot, we had a good chance of maintaining a fair degree of accuracy with our pistols. The tremendous firepower of our revolvers brought death and destruction to those Mexicans who faced us. Their sabers were useless against revolvers. They broke and galloped from the field.

Their departure opened the entire Mexican line to our attack. Lee's infantry poured a steady fire into the Mexican cavalry. Our men still possessed a fully loaded pistol and fresh horses. I ordered the bugler to sound recall. The regiment assembled on the flag. In moments they were formed for another attack.

"Bugler, sound the charge!" All two hundred mounted men swept down on the larger wavering Mexican line. Being assailed on two fronts, they fled the field. We had inflicted heavy casualties and suffered none.

Mexican troops which had infiltrated the buildings on either side of the road leading to the gate stopped the progress of the attack. Two infantry brigades were brought forward to dislodge them in heavy house to house fighting.

Lieutenant Ulysses S. Grant cleared a platoon of Mexican infantry from a church with a large bell tower south of the road. A single light howitzer was hoisted into the tower. The fire from this one gun proved very effective in clearing the path to the San Cosme Gate.

Since the cavalry attack had been repelled and the main army was approaching the gate, my regiment was detached to watch for counter-attacks on the American left flank. By late afternoon, the Stars and Stripes flew over the San Cosme Gate.

Pockets of resistance continued through the night. General Worth brought up field mortars. They were able to lob exploding shells with extreme accuracy into the disintegrating defenses of the bleeding city.

During the night, General Santa Anna resigned as President of Mexico and escaped the city with a large body of troops. The great city had fallen. By morning, American flags flew over every point of military significance. Isolated snipers and die-hard defenders were rooted out and killed. The largest city in North America was now in our hands.

22

September 14, 1847, Puebla, Mexico

SANTA ANNA HAD FLED the capital with eight thousand men. His only hope was to sever the American line of supply and reinforcements, and to isolate them in the capital while he raised a new army in the countryside to continue the war.

He sent half of his men with General Joaquin Rea to attack and harass the enemy supply lines. The other half he took with him to Puebla.

He was especially angry with Puebla. When he and his staff were fleeing the defeat at Cerro Gordo, the gates of Puebla had been closed to him. They denied him fresh horses, food or water. But when the Americans had approached, they had thrown the city open wide to them. It appeared not all Mexicans loved their dictator.

The Americans had made Puebla a major supply depot on the long overland trip from Vera Cruz to Mexico City. It was garrisoned by Lieutenant Colonel Thomas Childs and five hundred men.

The same day Mexico City fell, advance elements of Rea's guerilla forces made probing attacks against Puebla. The Americans had fortified a convent, another old defensive position known as Fort Loretto, and the sturdy citadel of San Jose.

Rea's forces attacked San Jose, but were easily repulsed. They did manage to drive off the garrison's herd of cattle. Rea's demand for surrender was declined.

On September 22, Santa Anna himself appeared before the city's defense and demanded their surrender. He received his reply when an American marksman placed a .50 caliber slug squarely under his horse, throwing clods and pebbles under the startled animal's belly. The war horse responded by bucking the great general off and dislodging his new wooden leg.

Enraged by the laughter from the fortress and the embarrassment before his own men, Santa Anna ordered his troops to storm the city. After hard fighting, the greatly outnumbered American garrison was finally able to drive back a determined Mexican assault. Santa Anna left enough troops to keep the Americans bottled up within the city walls, and headed out to intercept a relief column coming from Vera Cruz.

The diminished Mexican forces gave the Americans the opportunity to launch periodic sorties against the besieging forces. They were gradually able to chip away at key parts of the Mexican siege, and even recovered over twenty head of the stolen cattle to feed the hungry garrison and citizens.

On October 12, 1847, General Scott's main column was seen on the move just a few miles from Puebla. The remaining Mexican forces broke camp. Some found their way to join Santa Anna. Some joined Rea's guerrillas; but most just went home.

We set up camp at Puebla. Various units were sent to deal with isolated pockets of trouble. My companies made regular patrols against General Rea's guerillas.

We were ideally suited for close action cavalry raids. With

Colts blazing, we swept one camp after another off the map. Many were killed, a few surrendered, and some faded away into the countryside to join other guerilla bands or return to their families.

I had a letter waiting for me when we returned from a patrol in October. I had received only two others since we had left the Texas coast. I wondered how many others had been written and never delivered.

October 1, 1847

Dearest Aaron,

We hear that the war is going well and may soon be over. We are all well. David asks about you every day. Marcus and Lucius are doing a good job checking on me. The Adamson boys have worked hard and have been a joy to have around. It is like the old days when we had our own boys that age in the house. I had forgotten how much they eat. Parker and Kevin eat like starving wolves. David is very attached to all three of them.

The corn made a good crop and is in the cribs. The cotton looks like it will yield well. We are waiting for a killing freeze before we begin picking. I hope you are home in time to send it to market. If not, we will store it until then. The fields are not the only thing making a good crop. I had waited to tell you, hoping you would be home by now. I am far along with child and expect the baby will come sometime in mid-November. I am sorry now to have kept it a secret, but I did not want you worried about me.

We heard that Blake Lane was killed in battle. His widow and children have moved in with her parents, the Applewhites.

Remember, you promised to return home. I am counting on it. I don't know when I have been more lonely for you. I pray daily for you and the men from Navasota Landing.

All my love,

Nancy

I sat in stunned silence; another child! I had been homesick before now, but I wanted to be on the next ship bound for Texas.

––––––––––

Gray Jamison had adopted a half-starved mixed breed puppy that had wandered into camp. He greedily ate anything Gray fed him, and slept at his feet all night.

On returning from a patrol, Gray noticed the puppy didn't run to greet him as usual. He lay nervously by the tent. Gray picked him up to pet him. The puppy whined and licked Gray's face and mouth. He refused anything to eat or drink.

During the night, Gray felt the puppy get up. He noticed that it was staggering and walking sideways. He quickly picked up the puppy to see what was wrong. It growled viciously and bit Gray on the face and hand. There was a considerable amount of blood. He dropped the puppy and lit a lantern to look at his face and hand. As the light fell across the ground in front of the tent, he could see that the puppy was foaming at the mouth and baring his teeth. As Gray moved closer, it lunged at him, but lack of coordination caused it to stumble and fall.

Tanner and Logan got up to see what had caused the commotion.

"Gray, that dog's got rabies!"Tanner blurted.

Then the two friends noticed the bite marks on Gray's face and hand.

"Oh my God, he bit you! I'm gettin' Colonel Turner." Logan ran to my tent.

I arrived to see Gray sitting quietly on his cot with Tanner beside him. I looked at his face and hand, then turned to look at the sick little dog by lantern light. It lay foaming and convulsing on the ground.

"Corporal of the guard!"

"Sir?"

"Please quietly alert the camp that there will be a gunshot in a few minutes. I don't want to start a panic."

"Logan, you go find General Worth's surgeon."

I waited half an hour to let the sentries pass the word, then shot the rabid puppy. Tanner scooped it up with a shovel and took it outside of camp to bury it.

The surgeon assessed Gray's wounds. He accepted our diagnosis of rabies in the pup. "Son, have you been handling it every day?"

"Yes, sir."

"He's been licking you on the hands and face?"

"Just like always, sir. He even licked me in the mouth earlier tonight when he wasn't feeling good."

"Puncture wounds like this from a young pup's teeth are like needles. They go deep. I don't know how to sugar coat this, son. I'm just going to tell you straight up, I don't see any way you didn't get infected with rabies. There is no treatment."

"Is there nothing you can do?"

"I can give you some opium to keep you quiet. But toward the end, it is the most horrible thing you can imagine."

"How long do I have?"

"You're going to feel fine for about two weeks, then you're going to start having headaches, blurry vision, and be weak all over. From that point, things will go downhill pretty fast."

"Am I going to be a danger to my friends?"

"Not now. But later you may be. Son, do you have a friend you trust to do a really hard thing for you?"

"Sure, I've got friends I trust with my life." Then a look of dark recognition slowly came over him. "I could never ask a friend to do that for me!"

"I am truly sorry for you, young man. Send for me if you need me."

Two days later we broke camp as the main army prepared to return to Vera Cruz. There we would board waiting transport ships to take us back to Texas. General Scott sent our regiment far ahead to scout for trouble. The men were divided by platoons under their individual sergeants.

Sergeant Branam caught a whiff of wood smoke. He took his platoon to investigate. As they followed a faint trail, Mexican guerillas appeared all along a rocky ledge on their left. More Mexicans appeared from the brush to their right. They had been ambushed.

"Platoon, wheel right! Charge!"

Their only escape was to rush the attackers in the brush. Leaving their backs exposed to the men along the ledge, they raced headlong into the brush straight at their attackers.

Tanner Moore's horse was shot out from under him. He was pinned by one leg and could not get up. Gray wheeled his horse around and dismounted to help Tanner. Six Mexicans appeared from the thick brush with muskets and bayonets. Gray pulled one of the Colts from his saddle holster. As the men rushed at him, he dropped three men with three shots from his pistol. The others retreated into the cover of the brush.

Gray had to shoot the mortally wounded horse to stop it from thrashing and hurting Tanner even worse. He grabbed his childhood friend under the arms and began to pull him free. A musket fired from the brush hitting Gray in the right hip. He struggled to his feet and pulled harder, finally getting Tanner free. Just as he did, he was shot in the back through the ribs.

"Stay down." He gritted his teeth and grabbed the saddle pistols from Tanner's dead horse. He turned toward the brush and limped as fast as he could straight at the reloading soldiers. A musket fired, but missed him by just inches. He pushed on toward the guerrillas as they came at him with their bayonets. He raised both pistols and fired all twelve rounds, killing all three soldiers. As he fired the last shot, a rifle cracked on the ledge far behind him sending a bullet deep into his chest. His legs folded beneath him as he slumped face down on the ground.

Logan came galloping up. He caught Gray's horse and helped Tanner to mount. The two of them rode on either side of Gray's lifeless body and grabbed an arm. As a scattering of musket shots were fired from the ledge, they galloped to safety dragging Gray's body with them.

The last of the Mexicans scattered from the brush, and those on the rocky ledge disappeared. Two other platoons had rushed to their assistance, but found no one to fight.

Gray's body was returned to the regiment. He was buried near the road and a large pile of rocks was raised to mark the grave. I led the men in a brief prayer for our friend.

With General Scott's permission, Gray was promoted to lieutenant. At least Abigail would receive a small army pension of thirteen dollars a month.

23

November 15, 1847, Navasota Crossing, Texas

WE HAD DISEMBARKED from *Yellowstone* at Louisiana Landing at daybreak and ridden hard all day to get home. I went immediately to my house where Nancy waited for me on the porch holding a squirming bundle.

"Meet your son, Noah."

I wrapped my arms around Nancy and the baby and held them tight. I felt a persistent tugging on my pants and bent to scoop up David.

"Daddy's home! Daddy's home!"

"Yes, son. And Daddy's gonna stay home."

I unfolded the blankets to get a look at Noah. He had light blue eyes and a little bit of fuzzy red hair. I pulled him to my face and held him there. I was home.

Words wouldn't come for a while. I sat by the fireplace with Nancy and David. Little Noah slept in a cradle at my feet. When the words finally did come, it was like a flood. I told Nancy of so many things, as David hung on every word. I didn't know where to begin or where to end, I just talked.

On February 2, 1848, the Treaty of Guadalupe Hidalgo officially ended the war.

Mexico ceded all territory north of the Rio Grande. It was a vast area of over half a million square miles. It represented forty percent of Mexico's land area, but less than one percent of its population. Santa Anna was exiled to Jamaica. The United States paid Mexico $15,000,000 in reparations for the war and assumed all claims against Mexico.

The Stars and Stripes and the Lone Star flag flew side by side at our post office. Keeping my promise to Nancy, I resigned as commander of the militia. It was past time for me to stay home and let someone else do the fighting.

In the days and years that followed the war, I found peace and happiness at home. I worked my crops and raised good cattle, horses and mules. I continued to preach regularly. I kept my job as justice of the peace, and peace was what I found.

Our place beside the Camino Real along the Navasota River had become the paradise I had envisioned so long ago. I had found my "promised land." But the breeze in the cottonwood trees whispered of things to come. The water swirling slowly by in the river murmured a prophesy unheard by human ears. True and lasting peace would prove elusive. Many a sacrifice of Texas' sons and daughters would be required before Texas would know a lasting peace.

Epilogue

THE LAND WRESTLED from Mexico included all or part of the southwestern United States from the Gulf and the Rio Grande to the Rockies and west to the shores of the Pacific Ocean. Texas was marked as a land and people apart because of its unique history. Many of the men who fought shoulder to shoulder against Mexico would become prominent leaders in American history. Many of them would see our nation torn apart by a bloody civil war where they would lead brother in battle against brother.

Aaron Turner settled in the area described near the junction of the Camino Real and the Navasota River. He farmed and raised livestock and children on the land he loved there. He preached there until he died in 1851 at the age of sixty-eight. He would father one more child late in life, my great-grandfather, Aaron Lloyd Turner.

Nancy survived many more years. She saw David, Noah, and Aaron ride away to war in 1862. Only Noah and Aaron would return. In 1870, she sold the family land and moved gradually westward, finally settling in Callahan County.

The roots put down by Aaron Turner in the deep rich soil of Texas would sustain his family down to the seventh generation. This remarkable man left a legacy of goodness, decency and duty for his descendants. *On the Camino Real, Under Troubled Skies,* and *Ride for the Lone Star* are a tribute to a life lived well.

The life of his youngest son, Aaron Lloyd Turner, is honored in the next four books of this series: *On the Road to Glory, Up from the Ashes, On the Western Trail,* and *The Last Trail West.*

Glossary

Arroyo: a seasonal stream bed

Bearer bonds: bonds issued by a government, business, or financial institution that carried a specified face value plus a future interest payment to whoever presented them

Brogans: plain sturdy leather work shoes

Comancheria: the Comanche homeland and hunting grounds roughly defined on the west by the mountains of New Mexico, the Oklahoma panhandle on the north, the Rio Grande to the south, and the Brazos River on the east

Comancheros: those who traded with the Comanche, often for horses, guns, and captives; Comancheros came from northern Mexico and the eastern plains of New Mexico; they were often of Spanish or Mexican ancestry, but often included people of mixed race

Conscripts: those who are forced into military service by the government

Coup: (Coos) striking an enemy in combat, including killing them; in many cultures it was considered more honorable to strike a non-lethal blow against an enemy

Dally: to loop a rope over the saddle horn to allow the rope to play out slack to the roped animal, as opposed to "tying on" where the rope is tied to the horn; using a dally allowed the roper to slow the animal while "gathering slack"; "tying on" would stop an animal in their tracks when they hit the end of the rope, but at greater risk of injury to the roped animal; a large, heavy animal could hit the end of a rope hard enough to break its neck, break the rope or drag the saddle and rider off the horse

Drag: the position at the rear of a herd of driven animals; the dust was the worst here, and usually the least experienced riders were assigned to work in the drag position; alternative: to rope and drag an animal to be branded

Dragoon: mounted riflemen, often also carrying a saber

Duwali: also known as Chief Bowls; High Chief of the Cherokee in Texas and personal friend of Sam Houston

Escopeta: (es co pe' tah) a large smoothbore musket used by many countries, but particularly Mexico; they fired bullets from .54 to .79 caliber, with .69 being the most common; they were notoriously inaccurate beyond seventy yards; they were durable and heavy; they were ideal for use in close combat with a bayonet

Feint: a move or action taken to deceive the observer

Grama grasses: a large group of related native grasses found over much of North America

Guidon: a military banner identifying a specific military unit, usually small and made to be carried on horseback; guidons helped soldiers locate their unit in battle

Gyp: dissolved calcium containing minerals in water; it gives an off taste to water; it has a laxative effect, depending on the amount of dissolved minerals and the amount consumed; large amounts of strong gyp water could result in death to humans and animals

Labor: an old unit of Spanish land measurement equal to one hundred seventy-seven acres

Lancer: mounted soldiers armed with eight foot spears tipped with razor sharp metal points

League: an old Spanish unit of land measurement equal to four thousand four hundred and twenty-eight acres; also a distance of roughly 2.6 miles

Methuselah: the oldest man recorded in the Bible, over nine hundred years old

Nacogdoches: (nac ah doh' chez) important center of trade in eastern Texas on the Camino Real; one of the oldest cities in Texas, and for many years the largest city in eastern Texas

Natchitoches: (nac' ah tosh) an important center of trade in western Louisiana on the Red River; the Camino Real joined the Natchez Trace here

Neches River: an important River in east Texas that was the location of the "Cherokee Wars"

Nueces River: a river of more political than actual importance, angling northwest to southeast across western Texas; it was claimed by Mexico to be the southern border of Texas rather than the Rio Grande; in Spanish, nueces means "nuts" for the pecans that grew on the upper Nueces River

Reconnaissance: a military scouting or spying mission for the purpose of gaining information about the enemy

Refugio: (re few' e oh) a frequently contested town south of San Antonio

Riata: a braided rawhide rope, also spelled reata

Scrip: a paper substitute for other forms of money; land scrip was backed by a the right to claim actual land from the state of Texas, making it much more valuable and acceptable than other types of scrip

Section: a unit of land one mile square equal to six hundred and forty acres; also half section (three hundred and twenty acres); also quarter section (one hundred and sixty acres)

Travois: (tra' voy) two crossed poles dragged behind a horse for carrying people or goods

War bag: a multipurpose bag of leather or canvas for carrying a variety of materials, the type of bag a militia man might keep packed and ready if he were to be called to service

Whooping cough: a disease of children and adults caused by bacteria that cause symptoms ranging from a mild cold to respiratory collapse and death

Yellow fever: a devastating, widely feared disease, now known to be spread by mosquito bites, that causes very severe disease with high fever, severe body aches, bleeding, vomiting and frequently death; it was often called "the black vomit" for the symptom of vomiting digested blood; for centuries thought to be caused by person to person contact

Suggested Reading

Campbell, Randolph B. *Gone to Texas: a history of the Lone Star State*. New York: Oxford University Press. 2003

Cantrell, Gregg. *Stephen F. Austin, Empresario of Texas*. New Haven: Yale University Press. 1999

Fehrenbach, T. R. *Lone Star: A History of Texas and Texans* New York: Collier Books. 1968

Hardin, Stephen L. *Texian Iliad*. Austin: University of Texas Press. 1994

LaVere, David. *The Texas Indians*. College Station: Texas A&M University Press. 2004

Meyers, Michael C.; Sherman, William L.; Deeds, Susan M. *The Course of Mexican History, Seventh Edition*. New York: Oxford University Press. 1985

Miller, Robert R. *Mexico, A History*. Norman: University of Oklahoma Press. 1985

Newcomb, W.W., Junior. *The Indians of Texas*. Austin: University of Texas Press. 1985